as his partner, she knew he was ticked.

Lara sat back down on the low wall that bordered their flower beds and looked up at him. "No. I didn't."

At his snort, she gave him a look. "I really didn't, Matt. I've been defined my whole life by my bipolar mother and drug-addict sister. And for once, I just wanted to be me, on my own, no family giving everyone a reason to doubt me—or feel sorry for me."

He dropped his arms and came to sit by her on the wall. "I can understand that."

Matt's dad was the Emerald County Sheriff. He had a mom who not only knew how to cook, she did cook, and he and his two brothers were all superhero material from what she'd heard.

She stared at him. There was something, some sadness she couldn't quite quantify in his expression, but when she looked again, he smiled and whatever it was had disappeared.

"This really isn't about us, is it?" His voice had gone husky.

Books by Stephanie Newton

Love Inspired Suspense

*Perfect Target
*Moving Target
*Smoke Screen
*Flashpoint

*Emerald Coast 911

STEPHANIE NEWTON

penned her first suspense story—complete with illustrations—at the age of twelve, but didn't write seriously until her youngest child was in first grade. She lives in northwest Florida where she gains inspiration from the sugar-white sand, aqua-blue-green water of the Gulf of Mexico, and the many unusual and interesting things you see when you live on the beach. You can find her most often enjoying the water with her family, or at their church, where her husband is the pastor. Visit Stephanie at her Web site, www.stephanienewton.net, or send an e-mail to newtonwriter@gmail.com.

FLASHPOINT

STEPHANIE NEWTON

Steeple
Hill®

Published by Steeple Hill Books™

STEEPLE HILL BOOKS

Steeple
Hill®

Recycling programs
for this product may
not exist in your area.

ISBN-13: 978-0-373-67422-0

FLASHPOINT

www.SteepleHill.com

Printed in U.S.A.

You were saved by faith in God, who treats us much better than we deserve. This is God's gift to you, and not anything you have done on your own.
—*Ephesians* 2:8

For Jessi. I'm so blessed to have a sister and honored to call you my friend. I love you!

Thanks so much to Joe Reeder, firefighter/EMT with Bay County Fire-Rescue, and to his awesome wife, Becki, for taking the time to vet this book. What's right is due to Joe's technical expertise. Any mistakes or inconsistencies, those are all mine; Melissa Endlich, my fabulous and amazing editor; my family, who deal with long hours and odd Crockpot experiments—I love you; Catherine Mann, Brenda Minton and Holly La Pat. I wouldn't want to do this without you.

ONE

The flimsy door was no match for Matt Clark's boot. He kicked it in, ducking as the greedy fire sucked in fresh air. Heat surged toward him as he pushed into the front room, his partner, Lara Hughes, beside him. J.T. Keller and Miguel Santos were at the door behind them.

The house should be empty—on the foreclosure list according to property records. No one was supposed to be living here, but Matt had seen the overflowing trash cans baking in the hot summer sun, and the sleeping bags and uncovered mattresses on the floor of the living room added to the story. A story currently giving him the willies.

He caught Lara's eye. "I have a bad feeling about this."

"Tell me about it." Lara made one more visual sweep of the room, her voice tinny through the SCBA mask.

Smoke swirled in the room, a living, breathing thing. Around the edges of the swinging kitchen door, he could see a telltale orange glow and pulled the hose with him deeper into the house. The basics of firefighting. Put water on fire. "We're heading into the kitchen."

Matt barely registered the response over the heat that rushed them when he opened the door. He hit his knees, and beside him he felt more than heard Lara thump to hers. Obviously the center of the fire, the room glowed, every surface flaming or charred. The Sheetrock walls bubbled in some places and burned through in so many others that it was impossible to tell where the burn started.

The air too superheated for words, Matt motioned to Lara to stay down. He turned the nozzle to fire a stream through the nearest window, giving the hot gases a place to escape.

As the smoke cleared, they climbed to their feet. Matt took quick stock of the room. He laid the spray of water directly over the kitchen table. A conglomeration of objects remained, telling him that, although the residents of this house had definitely been cooking, they weren't using Grandma's cookbook.

They were cooking meth.

He ducked down to look under the table. And immediately knew that the heebie-jeebies he'd been fighting all afternoon had been seriously justified.

He started backing toward the door and turned to Lara. "Get out of here. This place is gonna blow."

She shook her head. "Another couple minutes and we'll have it under control."

"Another couple of minutes and we'll be dead. Get out of here. *Now.*"

She took off for the front door, the smoke billowing and closing around her. Close on her heels, he felt the intense heat bearing down on him. He could almost hear the clock ticking in his head. As he broke through the smoke, the force of the blast slammed into him—a physical blow—catapulting him into the air. He flew, arms and legs splayed all directions.

In that split second his thoughts fragmented.

His family. His sweet dark-haired mom. His county sheriff father. How he'd never get to see his old man be proud that his son had joined the Sea Breeze Police Department as their first-ever arson investigator.

And Lara.

The last thought as the ground raced toward

him was a wisp of a prayer that his beautiful, stubborn partner would be okay.

Lara Hughes blinked her eyes against too-bright sunlight. The sound of a PASS alarm found its way into her consciousness. Hers or someone else's?

She tested her legs and arms. All still attached. She tried to think back. She'd wanted to stay and fight the fire, but Matt had told her to get out.

Matt.

Struggling to a sitting position, she winced as pain shot up her arm. Todd Blankenship hoofed it across the lawn toward her, carrying a kit from the bus. It hadn't been more than a few seconds, then.

"I'm fine." She climbed to her feet, wavered, blinked to clear her head. Debris still rained down from the violent blast, soot and ash sifting to the ground. Todd grabbed her arm. She shook it off and stepped back. "I'm fine. Where's Matt?"

Blankenship gestured back at the house. At the base of the steps, Matt lay sprawled, paramedic Daniel Hudson at his side. She pulled out of Todd's grip and ran toward Matt, stripping off her gear as she went.

Behind them, Ladder 2 had arrived. The

crew was creating a spray over the top of the house—a place they all now knew had been a meth lab—trying to keep the fumes of ammonium hydroxide from spreading through the neighborhood.

Matt's PASS alarm trilled again. He still wasn't moving. He'd been so much closer to the blast than she. If she'd left when he'd first asked her to, maybe that would've given him the extra couple of seconds he needed to get away.

"Backboard!" Daniel yelled at whoever could hear him, and Todd came running with it.

She pulled her gloves off and stuffed them under her elbow, feeling under Matt's hood for his pulse. She, like most of the firefighters on their crew, also had EMT training. On their small crew everyone did double duty.

Where was it?

She moved her fingers. There. His pulse was there, strong and steady under her fingers. Why didn't he wake up? "Come on, Matt, open your eyes."

"Get him on the board." Daniel pulled Matt's SCBA gear off and rolled him to his back on the board, bracing his neck with a cervical collar. "Ready, go."

Todd and Daniel lifted Matt on the backboard

and moved him about fifty feet away from the extreme heat and toxic fumes of the still-burning house.

She dropped to her knees at his side as Daniel checked Matt's breathing. "Airway clear."

Lara smoothed dark black curls away from Matt's face. He was much more than a partner. He was a friend. "Come on, Matt."

Daniel shined a penlight on Matt's pupils. "Pupils equal and reactive."

That was something. *Okay. Okay. He's breathing on his own. Pupils aren't blown.* She took a deep breath and leaned in close to his ear. "Matthew Clark, stop being a baby and wake up."

He didn't move. She sat back on her heels, sweeping her damp sweaty bangs back from her forehead with a thick Nomex sleeve. It stung. She looked down and blinked. Her sleeve was smeared with blood.

Matt's eyes fluttered. "Lara, sweetheart. Kiss me. It hurts."

He opened his eyes, amusement winking in the dark brown of bitter chocolate. She slapped him on the arm with her gloves.

"Hey, what was that for? I nearly died. You can at least let me have a nice dream." A grin pulled at his lips, but underneath his tan, he was still pale, way more pale than he should've been. Concern knotted in her stomach.

She wouldn't let him see it, though. She didn't want him to know how badly he'd scared her. "I'll give you something to dream about, honey."

He laughed and pushed up to rest on his elbow, pain creasing the laugh lines at the edges of his eyes as he tested his range of motion. "You love me, you know you do."

She levered herself to her feet, used to the weight of the heavy suit. "Yeah, you and that overinflated ego of yours, too."

"She's gotcha there." Blankenship offered him a hand. "You all in one piece?"

Matt gripped Todd's hand and eased into a sitting position, gingerly moving his arms and legs, rubbing his forehead with a hand adorned with two pink Hello Kitty bandages. "Seem to be. Got one tangle of a traffic jam going on in my head, though."

Daniel activated an instant cold pack and handed it to Matt, then popped another one for Lara before pulling bandages from the kit. He quickly taped the cut on her head shut and placed the ice bag on it before packing the emergency gear back into the kit and taking the C-collar from Matt. "I suggest you both take a trip to the E.R. As hardheaded as you two are, a CT scan is still in order."

She held out a hand to Matt and pulled him the rest of the way to his feet, watching him closely as he swayed, his feet crunching in the dry summer grass. "You okay?"

"Fine." He shot her the grin that in the beginning had made her think he was a goofy show-off. He hadn't done much to dispel that image, always playing practical jokes in the firehouse. But it hadn't taken her long as his partner to see beneath that to the guy underneath who took his job very seriously.

Two in, two out. She'd always been tenacious, but sometimes it turned to a stubborn desire to be the best, to beat the fire. Today that stubbornness had almost caused her to forget that simple but most important rule of firefighting: *You go in with your partner. You come out with your partner.*

As the two medics walked away, she touched Matt's arm. "I'm sorry."

Surprise tinged his features. "We do what we do, Bump. It's no big."

At the nickname, she smiled. He'd dubbed her with it the first week she'd been in training because, unlike the men, she tended to use her hip as an extra appendage. It came from the days when her sister Emmy was an infant—she'd been a nine-year-old with a baby always in her arms because her mother wasn't around to take care of them. That hip came in handy.

A siren wailed to a stop outside the perimeter and a car door slammed.

He elbowed her. "Come on. That headache of yours isn't going to get you out of mop-up any more than mine is. And don't forget your gear. No going into this place without SCBA."

A self-contained breathing apparatus wasn't always necessary for overhaul, but in this case the toxic fumes associated with cooking meth made it dangerous to breathe without it. The nasty concoction of chemicals could kill. Their quiet beach town on the northwest Florida coast had seen its share of crime lately, but a meth lab right smack in the middle of a neighborhood… that was a new one, at least for her.

She found her mask and tank along with her helmet on the ground where she'd ditched them.

"Captain called in something about a meth lab fire?" Police lieutenant Chloe Rollins picked her way across the grass in high heels, the flash of myriad emergency lights flaring on her face.

Man-in-charge as the senior officer on-site,

Matt answered. "This place has definitely been used as a lab. If you're going in, you need gear."

"I've got it in the car." Chloe narrowed her eyes. "Looks like a bomb went off."

Matt nodded then grabbed his head. "That would be the propane tank, and the cause of the headache currently threatening to split my head in two. Gear up and I'll show you more inside, but we're probably not going to find much left, at least not in the kitchen."

The police lieutenant didn't move. Matt started for the house then glanced back. "What?"

Chloe grinned, her red hair gleaming in the sun. "Hello Kitty?"

Matt studied the bandages on his hand and shot her a cocky smile. "Dude, Hello Kitty rocks. It could be worse. Last week my neighbor's girls were into princesses. Sometimes she gets home after the bus drops the girls off. So I meet them at the bus stop, let them have a snack. They, uh, fix my boo-boos."

Guilt shot through Lara, a quick pang to the chest. She'd been working with Matt for two years and didn't know that about him. But she'd been the one to draw that line. Draw the boundaries between work life and home life. It wasn't that she didn't care.

She did.

But she couldn't be open in return and share the train wreck that was her life. She didn't want the guys—any of them—to feel sorry for her. "Sweet."

He made a face at her, then grinned at Chloe. "They're no trouble. They get a big brother who's a friend to their mom and I get somebody to water the plants when I'm gone. And all the free Hello Kitty bandages I want."

Chloe laughed.

"Yeah, go ahead and giggle, Lieutenant Rollins. You and Pastor Jake'll probably have triplets."

Chloe's face drained of color. Her hand went to her stomach. "Bite your tongue."

Matt pulled his mask over his face and hollered at J.T. and Santos, who were hanging out by the rig. "Let's go, you slackers." To the cop he said, "Get your gear on and we'll meet you in the house."

Lara pulled her own mask into place, the snug straps making her aching head throb even worse. She followed Matt into the burned-out shell of a house. What had once been a fairly nice home was a smoking ruin. The mattresses and sleeping bags were melted into a charred mess. The remnants of the walls and ceilings would be coming down, too. Nothing could remain that might be hiding a smoldering hot spot.

Water dripped from the ceiling to form toxic puddles in the soggy carpet.

"We'll take the kitchen." Matt's eyes met Lara's. She nodded. She had to put their close call out of her mind. Facing the fear was part of what they did every single day. "Santos, you and J.T. start in the front room and we'll all work our way back through the bedrooms."

The detective in her white hazmat suit followed them into the kitchen—or what was left standing in the kitchen. The entire back wall had blown away, leaving the back steps and very little else recognizable.

"Whoa." The word was barely a breath as Lara realized what would have happened to them if they'd still been in the room when it blew.

"Yeah." Matt looked around. "Well, I think we can safely say there's no fuel left in here. Everything's already in the backyard."

She turned away from the wreckage in the kitchen, taking in a tight breath. "Let's hit the front room, then. I'm ready to get out of here."

Chloe stood in the doorway with her digital camera. "What a mess. We're gonna need statements from you guys about what you saw—before the blast."

In the front room, J.T. and Santos tossed debris out the front door. It was a pile of tattered sleeping bags, and what Lara had managed to push to the back of her mind shoved back to the forefront again. Had her sister lived in a place like this? Had Emmy been so desperate for the drug that she'd been willing to poison herself to get it?

"Hey, Lara. You okay?" Matt looked into her face mask. "That bump on the head got you a little loopy?"

As her partner and friend, he would support her if he knew about her family, as would the other guys. But they would never look at her the same way again. She'd always be the daughter of a mother who showed up drunk for her school play and the sister of a drug addict. She'd always be the one who had to raise her sister and never just a firefighter who did her job well.

She shoved the pain away and picked up her shovel. "I'm fine."

Fine. Yeah, right. Matt watched as Lara nearly visibly shook off whatever was bothering her and turned to J.T. and Santos, who were starting on the drywall. Already damp and damaged, it tore away in chunks.

But he'd given up trying to get beneath that hard exterior of hers, right? After one really bad argument about a year ago now, they'd almost decided to call it quits as partners. And he'd had to choose. Be her friend and let her have her secrets, or try to force her to talk and lose her forever.

It wasn't a hard decision. Her friendship was important to him. Being her partner and knowing there was pain hiding behind those pretty hazel eyes, that was harder.

Behind his mask, he started whistling "Smoke on the Water." Lara rolled her eyes at him but after a second joined in on the chorus with a half laugh as they pulled huge pieces of the wall away. As she tore the base of the drywall away, she stopped midwhistle.

Matt took a look into the space between the studs. "That's an impressive collection someone's been hiding. Chloe, I think you may want to take a look at this."

The police lieutenant stepped across the piles of debris, peered into the hole and lifted her camera to take a shot. "I wasn't expecting to find that here."

She clicked through several more frames,

then stepped forward to take one more closer picture. "All right, pull down the rest of the wall. Carefully."

Matt pulled the rest of the wall away, chipping at the last little bit and tossing the entire mess onto the pile into the middle of the room for removal. In the space between the wall and the one behind it sat six highly illegal, brand-new submachine guns. He stepped farther back so Chloe could get a closer look.

"I don't think you can get those outside the military." Chloe snapped another few photographs, then turned to look at the firefighters. "Anybody heard when Fuentes is supposed to be on scene?"

When she got no response, Lieutenant Rollins lifted her walkie-talkie to her face mask, walking toward the front door as she talked.

Lara pulled a piece of drywall from the next panel but called back to Chloe. "We're gonna need to take this whole wall down. Do you want me to keep pulling or wait for the Crime Scene Unit?"

Rollins waved her on. "Go ahead, but let's try to keep this section separated from the rest of the debris. The CSU will have to process it. They'll be here in five."

As Lara punched a hole in the wall, Matt

started pulling it down. When he saw metal cases stacked between the studs, he stopped and again motioned the cop forward.

Chloe brought her Nikon closer, snapping photos. "More guns?"

Matt shrugged, checking his air meter as the alarm began to beep. "Or maybe money."

Lara pulled the rest of the wallboard away and tossed it into the growing pile. "I didn't think meth dealers made that much money."

"Most of them don't because they're too busy getting high. They neglect their kids, their property, their jobs—if they can keep them. It's a waste." Chloe shook her head, looking at the submachine guns, her gaze wary. "No, this is definitely something bigger than just a couple of tweakers looking to make some extra money on the sly."

Maria Fuentes, Sea Breeze Police Department's forensic specialist, shoved through the door with her kit, looking like some kind of alien in light blue hazmat gear. "What've we got here?"

Matt swept his arm around the room, game-show style. "Take your pick, Fuentes. There's your basic damaged evidence, contraband weapons, some unidentified…something in metal cases, and so far, no clue who to tie it to."

Maria grinned behind her mask. "Well, we'll just have to see about that, won't we?"

Lara's low-air alarm beeped, creating a tandem harmony with Matt's. She glanced at her gauge. When she dropped it, Matt picked it up and checked it himself.

Lara was doing the job, but she was being just a little too careful about how she moved. He wanted to get her out of here. Matt cleared his throat. "If you're going to be busy here awhile…"

Maria Fuentes glanced up. "Go. We've got this. If we need a superhot firefighter, we know where to find you."

"A-ha-ha. You're so funny, Fuentes."

Lara beelined for the door. Bypassing the piles of Sheetrock and debris, she stepped onto the front porch. She jerked the buckles of her coat open.

Matt came out behind her, pulling off his mask and letting it hang over his shoulder. "Hey, seriously, you okay?"

"I'm fine, I just needed some air." She leaned against the column of the porch.

He studied her face, still not happy with her color. "You know, officially our shift is over. Since the crew from Ladder 2 is here to help, I don't think anyone would object to us going to the E.R. to get both our heads x-rayed."

A tired smile lifted the corner of her lips. "You need your head checked, Clark."

He fake punched her arm. "Yeah, maybe they'll discover there's actually a brain in there, you never know. Let me toss this gear and see if I can finagle the keys to Captain Caruso's truck."

As he walked away, he saw her shoulders sag. There was something going on—something that he needed to know. Because personal space or not, she was his partner. And in his world, partners were there for each other.

Lara dumped her SCBA and carefully eased down the steps, every muscle in her body making itself known with twinges and aches, even the occasional sharp pain. She forced out a breath through airways that suddenly seemed too constricted to breathe. It really had been close. And if she'd stayed in that house to fight, she wouldn't have survived. She'd have been in little pieces like all the stuff in the backyard that Maria Fuentes's crime-scene unit would be collecting. And so would her partner.

Lara walked away from the noise—dozens of cops and firefighters worked a fire scene. More came as spectators. She just needed a minute to get her head on straight.

As she rounded the corner toward what remained of the back of the house, she carefully stepped over the debris. And as she got a good look at the view from the back—an empty shell, the roof blown away to expose charred beams—she stopped cold.

Did Emmy live in a place like that?

Did her baby sister live in a pile of trash like they'd seen when they went in, breathing in toxic fumes? Every moment a new chance for disaster? Or did she live her life scrambling to scrape up the money for the next hit, the next high?

A sound popped behind her. She turned to see a man picking through the debris in the backyard. Tall and thin, with thick black hair and glasses, he looked more like he belonged in a laboratory than at a crime scene.

Probably one of Fuentes's guys.

As she watched, he lifted his head and caught sight of her. She lifted her hand to wave, but he didn't meet her eyes. He picked up a piece of evidence and disappeared around the side of the house. She shook her head. There was a reason some of those guys did better in the lab.

She trudged back to the front of the house.

Matt was nowhere to be seen. She tossed her turnout coat onto the seat of the rig and picked up a cup, filling it with water from the container they carried.

Sweat had her T-shirt stuck to her back and bangs plastered to her forehead. She resisted the urge to pour the water onto the top of her head.

Fuentes walked up beside her, unzipping the top half of her suit. "Whew, can't stay in there much longer than that without getting completely claustrophobic."

Lara filled another cup without asking and wordlessly handed it to the CSI, who drained it in one gulp.

"Thanks."

"So what's your guy looking for in the backyard?" Lara eased her bright red suspenders off her sore shoulders.

Maria shoved back a flyaway curl. "What guy? The only one working today is Paulie, and he was working in the bedrooms where there was less damage."

"Tall, black hair…"

The crime-scene investigator raised a quizzical eyebrow. "Nope."

The heat drained from Lara's face. "But if he wasn't with you, then…"

Fuentes jumped to her feet and whistled for one of the uniformed cops. He met her on the street and after a few words went running for the backyard, calling for another officer to join him.

Maria walked back toward Lara, her mouth set in a serious line. "He was probably looking for a way into the house. There's at least quarter of a million dollars in those cases and more money in the guns, not to mention a lot more on the line if we catch them. He'd likely be willing to risk quite a lot to get that evidence out of our hands."

Lara collapsed onto the running board of the rig, her legs rubbery. "I saw him. I waved to him."

"Can you describe him to a sketch artist?" Maria crumpled the cup in her hand and tossed it on the growing pile of debris on the front lawn.

Slowly, Lara nodded, her stomach twisting in knots. She had a dangerous job. She'd fought hard to be one of only two female firefighters in Emerald County. But, even so, she took calculated risks that she was completely prepared for.

Right now, she couldn't help but think she'd jumped into the fire with the big boys.

Without a hose.

TWO

The intense light seared the back of Matt's already aching eyes. Away and back. The pounding in his head increased.

The doctor moved away to look at the films on the computer screen. "How long were you unconscious?"

"I'm not sure. Thirty seconds or a minute probably."

"Memory loss?" The guy in the white coat didn't look at him. Was that a bad sign?

"I don't remember actually hitting the ground. I remember what happened before and after." Sort of.

The doctor pulled reading glasses off his face and turned to face Matt. "You've got a concussion, probably just a mild one, but you shouldn't be alone tonight. Any loss of consciousness should be considered serious. If your headache gets worse or your vision gets blurry, get back to the emergency room immediately."

Matt started to nod then remembered it hurt. "Sure thing."

He slid off the exam table, landing his feet on the floor and leaving his suspenders to hang. He started for the door. "Sir? My partner?"

The doctor flipped some water off with his elbow and reached for a paper towel. "Next door."

"Thanks."

The door to the next exam room stood ajar. Matt poked his head into the room. Sitting on the high table, Lara had her eyes closed as another doctor sutured the cut on her forehead. His partner looked way more white and fragile than she should, the stitches stark and black against her skin.

He was so used to Lara looking strong and capable. But in the hospital room, with stitches against her skin, it struck him how close they'd actually come to losing it today. To losing everything. Those prayers his mom was always praying must've been working overtime today.

Even in her dirty gear, her hair still in a lopsided ponytail, blood drying on her face, Lara was beautiful. He forgot that sometimes. But today, that place inside him that always wanted to take care of every hurt with his family and friends wanted to take care of her. To take care of what caused those shadows in her eyes.

What caused her to keep it all bottled up inside.

The nurse turned for the suture scissors and caught sight of him in the door. She whisked in a breath, her expression telling him exactly what she was about to say.

At the sound, Lara opened her eyes. The hazel color, as changeable as the sea, glinted green in the stark-white hospital room. She sighed and motioned him in.

The doctor made one last clip with the scissors before cleaning around the cut with an alcohol pad. Lara's lips tightened, but she didn't move.

Finally the nurse covered the stitches with a bandage and handed Lara a sheet of paper. "You know the drill. Read the sheet and if you have any questions, call us, okay?"

She rolled up her supplies and followed the doctor out of the room.

Matt didn't move from his position holding up the wall as the door whooshed slowly shut.

"Hey." Lara swung her feet off of the gurney.

"Hey, yourself." He walked over to her and

examined her sutures. "I'm pretty sure I can hook you up with a better-looking bandage."

"I want a princess one."

"You got it." He dropped into the chair beside the exam table. "You ready to break out of this joint?"

"Definitely. You driving?" She slid off the gurney onto the floor.

"Definitely. Doc doesn't want me to be alone. Did he give you the same talk?"

She made a face. "Yeah."

"I could crash on the couch if you want."

"Thanks, but my mom is…staying with me for a while. She can check on me." She turned her back on him, but her voice was hesitant.

"I didn't know your mom was in town."

Lara gingerly pulled her suspenders up over her shoulders. "I'm gonna be sore tomorrow."

"Looks like you already are." She was changing the subject just like she always did when they got too close to her family, to her past.

He followed her out of the E.R., the big glass doors sliding silently open in front of them. Lara pulled her ponytail out as soon as they walked outside. "Headache?"

"Yeah, I guess that's what I get for following you into burning buildings."

He laughed, but his chest ached. What would

it take to get past that wall? And why did he try so hard?

Maybe he just liked a challenge.

Maybe because she was brave and funny and one of the coolest people he'd ever met.

They had a dangerous job, but they did everything they could to minimize the danger. On a good day, everything went fine. Today, he and Lara had come really close to death.

He was going to do everything in his power to make sure that never happened again.

At her cottage home, Lara stepped out of the captain's truck onto the street. A car whizzed by. Too close.

She jumped back onto the curb, landing on her hip.

"You okay?" Matt was at her side in less than a second.

Her hand was at her neck, her heart pounding. How many close calls did one person get in a day?

"Yeah, I think." She let Matt pull her to her feet. She shook off the unease, shook off the fear. "I really need to take some ibuprofen and go to bed. I'll see you tomorrow."

"Uh-uh. I'm walking you in. You were hurt and some maniac just missed running you over.

No way you're going in on your own. My mom raised me better."

She hesitated, then waved him forward.

"You know, it's weird." Matt muttered it under his breath as he came toward her, but she was used to listening to his thoughts, at fires and after, as he tried to put the pieces together of why it started and where.

"What's weird?"

"I could've sworn I saw that same exact car in the parking lot at the hospital."

She stalled in the middle of the walk, her feet feeling like forty-pound weights. "Did you see the driver?"

"No. Probably nothing." His long, loping steps carried him easily up the sidewalk, the lavender lantana swaying in the breeze as he passed.

"Probably." She dug in her bag for the keys, that icky feeling of premonition settling in her stomach.

Before she could put her key in the lock, the door flew open and her mom stood framed there, a slim silhouette against the brighter lights of the living room. "I was worried when you didn't get home right after your shift. Oh, Lara, you're hurt."

Lara reached for the bandage on her head as yet another layer of guilt slapped on top of the many she carried around every day, for the years of letting things slide, status quo. Rationally, she knew she'd done the best she could—she'd been a kid. But in her gut, she believed—wished?—she could've done more. "I should've called. It's nothing."

Matt stepped up behind Lara. "She needs looking after tonight, Mrs. Hughes."

Lara's mom sent Matt a tremulous smile. She looked so young in her fuzzy robe and blond ponytail. She *was* young, had been a baby herself when she'd had Lara.

Lara sighed. "Mom, this is Matt. We work together."

"It's nice to meet you. And I'm not Mrs. Hughes. Please call me Ava." She brushed long bangs out of her eyes with graceful fingers.

Lara searched her face. She seemed to be so normal, seemed to be holding it together. But was it real?

"So why does my daughter need looking after?"

A protest formed on Lara's lips and she must've made some sound because Matt sent her an "I mean business" look that he usually reserved for the probies. She walked away instead, into the kitchen for a Diet Coke, battling back the sigh that seemed determined to find the surface.

It was her own fault. She'd known when she let him bring her home that she was inviting trouble. Taking her soda, she climbed the back stairs to change out of her grimy work clothes and take a quick shower. Hopefully, Matt would be gone when she came back downstairs. Hopefully, her mother wouldn't have said anything embarrassing and hopefully, she could go to bed and put this miserable day behind her.

After cleaning up, she opened the door of her bedroom and immediately heard Matt's big laugh, the sound sweet and full. But it was her mother's laugh that stopped her. When was the last time she'd heard it?

She stepped into the living room. Matt's feet were propped on the coffee table and he balanced a sandwich on his lap, a soda in a glass beside him.

Her living room was the polar opposite of the firehouse. No leather recliners here. Her style was more Pottery Barn knockoff, beachy colors and natural fibers. Yet somehow, Matt looked right at home.

Her mom sat in the chair opposite him, her cheeks pink.

Lara stood there for a long moment watching,

eyes stinging. With a start, she rubbed them. She had a head injury. The doctor had explained that she might have rapid mood changes. Which obviously explained her overly emotional response tonight.

Matt glanced up and caught sight of her. "Well, Hughes, you look slightly better than you did ten minutes ago. But you need food. Come on, your mom made you a sandwich, too."

Her mom taking care of her, now that *was* a switch.

"Thanks."

Matt patted the sofa beside him. She eased into the seat and her mom placed the sandwich beside her. She took a bite. Ham with honey mustard, her favorite. Her eyes searched out her mom. She hadn't even realized Ava knew.

"So, Ava, Lara tells me that you're staying here for a while. Where do you live?"

Her mother didn't answer the question, so Lara swallowed the knot of sandwich lodged in her throat. "Mom hasn't been well. She's just staying here until she's on her feet."

Lara accepted that she would probably always make excuses for Ava, considering she'd been doing it since childhood. *My mom isn't able to come to the parent meeting because she has to work. My mom isn't feeling well, that's why she stumbles when she walks. My mom is an actress, that's why she says weird things. She's practicing for a role.*

Every now and then when her mother would actually take her meds, she'd act normal for a while. Just long enough for Lara to hope that maybe she'd have someone to help her with her homework or that her mom might actually remember that it was her birthday. But it never lasted.

Ava fiddled with the ties on her fleece robe, wrapped almost double around her slight figure. "I've never really settled down, Matt. Just kinda bounced around. But I like Sea Breeze and I'd like to get an apartment near Lara, if she wouldn't mind."

"Of course I wouldn't mind, Mom." To her horror, Lara's eyes filled. She jumped to her feet. "Come on, I'll walk you to the door, Matt."

His brown eyes held questions, but he put his empty plate on the end table and slowly placed one booted foot, then the other on the floor. "Thanks for the sandwich, Ava."

"You're welcome anytime." Ava picked up the plates and disappeared into the kitchen as Matt and Lara stepped onto the front porch.

Lara scowled. "You're not welcome anytime.

I have to deal with you at the station house. I'm not living with you the rest of my life, too."

Just outside the door, he stopped. "What's your problem, Lara? Your mom is nice. She made me a sandwich. I get that you want to keep your personal life private, but give me a break. At some point, people's lives intersect. And if your mom is moving to Sea Breeze, we're bound to run into each other."

Lara dropped onto the bench beside the front door. She was beyond exhausted, her aching body and head making it difficult to think. And just like she'd eventually figured out as a kid, she was too tired to keep pretending that she had a normal life like everyone else. "My mom's bipolar, Matt. She's decided to work with her doctors instead of against them for now, and she's doing great." To her horror, her voice hitched.

With effort, she steadied it. "It's only been a few months. I want to make sure that it's for real before I start having backyard barbecues and inviting the crew over. We've been down this path before." Too many times to count.

Matt crouched in front of her and to his credit, he didn't even whimper, despite the fact that he had to be as sore as she was. "I'm sorry."

"Not your fault. Not anybody's fault, really."

His eyebrows pinched together. "I know, but you could've told me."

And have him feel sorry for her? No thanks. "I'd really rather people get to know me for me. Instead of all that." She waved a vague hand at the house.

He took her hands, his big and rough, hers smaller but no less hardened. "Is there more?"

She sighed. "There's always more, Matt. Didn't you learn that in your investigations class?"

Obviously deciding to let it go, he released her and stood. "We'll talk later?"

As she hesitated, a car turned the corner, its lights flaring across the porch. Matt narrowed his eyes and walked to the porch rail to get a better look.

"What is it?"

Matt shook his head, then grabbed his forehead. "I've got to remember not to do that. I just thought I saw that car again, but I'm probably hallucinating."

Lara went still. "Did you see the driver this time?"

"Um, black hair, skinny face, glasses?"

Her first instinct was to keep it to herself, that protective shell she used to hide kicking in. But it couldn't be a coincidence and Matt was her partner. If he'd seen the guy driving the car, it was possible that the driver had seen him, too. "It sounds like the same guy I saw sneaking around the crime scene this afternoon. I thought he was one of Fuentes's guys, but he wasn't."

Matt's voice was deceptively calm, the voice he used when things were tense in a fire. "And you're just telling me this now?"

Again she fought the urge to run away from him, from the tangle of emotion that he seemed to effortlessly pull from her. "I wasn't keeping anything from you. It just didn't come up."

He paced to the edge of the porch and back, his natural response to a stressor. She'd seen him do it a thousand times at the station house. "Not once in the four hours we spent in the emergency room and not once on the drive home could you have maybe told me that you saw one of the people connected to some very serious crimes?"

"Apparently not." She stood and walked over to him, grabbing the hand that had dropped hers. "But you're right. I should have told you. Especially since you're going to be investigating."

"You don't know that."

"What better person to work with the police department to find who's doing this? Captain Conyers has been waiting for the right case and for you to finish your training. This is it. It's the perfect case for the first-ever arson investigator on the Sea Breeze police force." She leaned against the porch rail beside him.

"We'll see. There are still some hoops to jump through. Namely getting approval from the chief of police."

"But since he's friends with your dad, it should be a piece of cake, right?"

"Yeah. Piece of cake." Matt pushed away from the railing and pointed to the door. "Inside, miss. To bed with you. Take care of that hard head of yours."

"And you?" She hesitated at the door.

"I'll be fine. I'll go sleep on my mother's lumpy couch."

She wanted to smirk at him, but something in his tone stopped her. She blinked at him, her partner, her friend. "Thanks for having my back today."

"All the way to wall." He held out a fist and she bumped it with a laugh.

"See ya." She closed the door. Sometimes she did wish things could be different. That she had a normal family, a normal life that she wanted to share with other people. It hadn't been too long ago when Matt had told her over coffee that he'd like to take her out on a real date.

He'd scared the living daylights out of her. She'd walked away from him and had almost blown their friendship that day.

But sometimes in the darkness of her room at night, with no one to even hear her thoughts except God—and if He knew anything, He wasn't telling—she might imagine that she'd gone on that date. That she'd let Matt take her to a restaurant and that he'd pulled the chair out for her. That he'd brought her flowers and held her hand under the table.

She wasn't really the type to be romanced.

She was fine with that. She had to be. And she *liked* her life…now. God had blessed her with health and friends and she didn't take it for granted.

But sometimes she wished…

Lara threw the dead bolt and leaned against the door. Tomorrow morning she would meet with the sketch artist to describe the man she'd seen at the meth lab in hopes that it would help the police find him. They needed answers.

She heard a car drive by outside and shivered.
These were dangerous people.
And they knew where she lived.

THREE

A hand on Matt's shoulder shook him awake. He didn't open his eyes. He knew that hand. "Mom, what are you doing?"

"Do you know your name?"

"Matt Clark. Mom, seriously."

"Who's the president?" She pried open his right eye and shined a flashlight into it.

"I know who the president is." He pulled the pillow over his face.

She peeled the cover back and levered open his left eye. "When's your birthday?"

"April 5. Why are you doing this?"

"You're the youngest of three boys, Matthew. Do you honestly think this is the first concussion I've treated?" She sat back on her heels beside the sofa. "Though it would've been nice if you'd called from the hospital. Or woken me when you got home. I don't like hearing about these things through the grapevine. An explosion, Matt?"

He sat up, feeling new aches and pains in muscles he wasn't sure he knew existed before today. "It wasn't that close a thing. We got out okay. I didn't want to worry you."

"And yet, here you are on my couch because you aren't supposed to be alone after a head injury." She got up and walked toward the kitchen, calling back over her shoulder, "No, really, it's fine. I'm not worried."

He followed her, taking a peek outside. It was pitch-black. "What time is it?"

"Four a.m. I woke you at two also. You don't remember?"

If he said no, he was on the fast train back to the E.R. "Of course I do."

"You've never been very good at lying to me, Matt." She tucked her still-dark hair behind one of her ears and reached for the coffeepot.

"Why aren't you asleep?"

"Can't sleep when I'm worried." She poured a cup of coffee. "Want some?"

He reached into the cabinet for a mug and held it out, hoping to goodness it wasn't that French vanilla stuff she liked.

She poured him a mug of black coffee, and he put his lips to the edge of the cup.

"And Lara?"

The scalding-hot brew singed his throat as he gulped it down. "Lara?"

"Your partner, Lara. You remember her." His mother stirred sugar into her coffee. How did she manage the executive look in pajamas and robe?

He narrowed his eyes. "She's fine."

"When are you going to bring her over for dinner?"

What could only be described as a pang hit Matt dead center. "I'm not, Mom. She's really not interested."

"How do you know that?"

His mother had an IQ of 148 and was the administrator of the largest hospital in the area. She knew good and well how he knew and if she didn't, she could figure it out. "She's made it very clear that she doesn't want any kind of personal relationship outside the job. It's her choice."

"Do you think so?" She took a ladylike sip of her coffee, her dark brown eyes perceptive and sharp.

"Yes, Mom, I do. I asked her to dinner a few months ago and it nearly wrecked our working relationship."

"Oh, honey. She said no?" She sat her coffee

mug down on the countertop with a clank, shaking the picture frames she had tucked into every nook and cranny.

"She not only said no, she threatened to transfer to another house if I asked her out again." It made his stomach hurt to think back to that day, when she walked away from him at the coffee shop. The closed expression on her face, the absolute shock when he'd asked her out. It had taken him months to break through the shell she'd erected and regain his footing with her. He wasn't going there again.

The expression on his mother's face turned cunning. "Well, that changes things, then, doesn't it?"

"No, it really doesn't." He walked to the sink and poured out the remainder of his coffee. "I'm going to head home."

His mom, who had been a cop's wife for thirty years, turned her youngest son toward her. "Be careful, Matthew. We've been seeing more cases at the hospital lately."

He stopped on his way to the door. "Drug cases?"

"Overdoses. We've heard a rumor that a new drug is being produced. More potent than meth and more addictive. I'm afraid that yesterday was only the start of what you'll be seeing. Promise me you'll be careful. These people mean business when it comes to making money."

"Today's my day off, Mom."

She gave him the look that had stopped him in his tracks as a little boy and even as an adult made him take notice.

"Okay, I promise I'll be careful."

"Tell Lara I asked about her."

He grinned. "I love you, Mom."

"I love you, too."

Closing the door gently, he stepped out the back door. Outside, the sky was still dark, the salty ocean breeze balmy. It would be a scorcher of a day later on.

He looked around. The play gym where he and his brothers had received a few of those concussions was a silent skeleton in the backyard. Underneath it was white beach sand where he, Ethan and Tyler had buried a thousand treasures. Those were the good memories. He hadn't seen Tyler in three years. And his brother Ethan, well, Ethan had his own skeletons to deal with.

His phone buzzed in his hand. He opened the text message from Police Captain Cruse Conyers. Meeting in twenty. My office.

Now that was interesting. Cruse wasn't waiting for the official approval to bring him in on the case.

It wasn't exactly a surprise to hear—more drugs on the street, more lethal than ever.

But after yesterday, his crew would have to be even more aware of their surroundings as they entered a fire scene. Or their near miss would be repeating itself with deadly consequences.

Lara walked into the three-story gray metal police station at five in the morning and followed the scent of fresh-brewed coffee to the third floor. Not normally a coffee drinker, she needed an infusion of caffeine. Her mother, who had never in her life been a nurturer, had apparently become convinced that she alone was responsible for Lara's well-being through the night.

Really, she didn't blame her mother. Matt on a good day was pretty hard to say no to. And Matt, weary and rugged after a long day on the job, was darn near impossible to resist.

"You're supposed to be resting." The deep voice behind her ear startled her.

Clean-shaven, his hair still damp around his face, Matt smiled, shoulder leaning against the institutional gray wall, a cup of coffee in his right hand.

"So are you." She tipped her own disposable cup at him. "Cheers. Conyers call you in?"

He nodded. "But I'm pretty sure I'll get more rest sitting in this meeting than I did at home. My mom woke me up every two hours."

She fought back a chuckle. "Mine, too, thanks to you."

Captain Conyers entered the precinct room, tired circles deepening to black under his bottle-green eyes. "If you'll all join me in the conference room, we'll get started. I apologize for the early hour, but we have some new information and we need everyone involved in this investigation up to speed as quickly as possible."

Before they could even take a seat around the large table, Cruse gave Maria Fuentes the floor. She clicked a PowerPoint slide onto the screen, a photo of a burned-out structure. "As you know, there was an explosion at a residence on Billfish Drive yesterday afternoon. At first the home appeared to be just another meth lab, which isn't that unheard-of these days. The materials are cheap and the drug methamphetamine is far too easy to manufacture."

She glanced at her notes, then clicked another slide. "Upon further exploration at the scene, we found military-issue assault weapons and upward of a quarter of a million dollars in small, untraceable bills."

One of the police officers interrupted as he waved a hand at the photo of the weapons. "That's not normal for a meth lab. Tweakers are usually too focused on getting to the next high to worry about future profit."

Gabe Sloan cut in. "Or to hang on to what profit they have."

Fuentes nodded, one springy curl loosening from her ponytail to bounce around her face. "Exactly. All of which made us determined to figure out what made this house different. And here's what we found when we analyzed the evidence we found from the actual lab."

She clicked another slide onto the screen. "The top graphic is methamphetamine. The bottom graphic is an unknown substance, very similar in chemical makeup, but it's one we've never seen before."

She clicked through to another slide. "Hospital stats of overdoses are up, leading us to believe that there is a new, very potent, very dangerous drug in the pipeline here. The amount of money and the hardware found at the scene make it likely that this is not a local operation. We also found equipment packed in boxes in one of the back rooms that made it seem probable that these criminals, whoever they are, were planning to set up a superlab right here in our town."

Lara sat very still, her hands twisted into a knot in her lap.

Cruse Conyers stood. "Thank you, Maria. Obviously, you are all here as part of the task force that will be working this case. Matt Clark and Lara Hughes will serve as the fire department liaisons and will be working with Maria to track the evidence from the fire. Gabe, you and Sheehan will be on the streets, tracking leads. We need to ask questions, but we need to keep a lid on this as long as possible in order to build a case and find the people responsible for bringing this into our town."

He looked around the room. "Anything else?"

One of the police officers raised a hand. "Sir, are we gonna bring outside agencies in on this one?"

Cruse nodded. "Good question. Yes, the DEA will be sending someone to assist and provide resources as soon as that person is available." He looked around. "If there's nothing else, then get busy. Let's get this drug off our streets."

Maria Fuentes collapsed into the chair next to Lara as soon as it was vacated.

"You look tired."

Maria barked a laugh. "My left arm for a nap."

Lara pulled her cold cup of coffee close. She stared into the cup. She didn't feel like drinking it. Not anymore. "I'm not exactly sure why I'm here."

"We need as many people as possible running down these leads. You're smart and you and Matt are used to working together. That will help. I have a feeling things are going to get tense before this is over."

Tense. That seemed like the understatement of the year. "So, you want me to work with the arson investigator." Saying it that way gave her the distance she needed. Just any other investigator.

"After you give the sketch artist the info about the man you saw. That's the closest thing we have to a lead so far." Maria closed her eyes.

"I saw him again." Lara looked into the muddy coffee in her cup. "Or Matt did."

Maria's eyes snapped open.

Lara looked up at the doorway to the conference room where Matt lounged, deep in conversation with Cruse Conyers. "A car followed us home from the hospital. From Matt's description, it was the same guy."

"We need that car." Maria pushed back from the table, her customary energy back in full force. "See the artist about the sketch and then work with Matt. Every lead. Not to be melodramatic or anything, but this is as big as it gets. The potency of this drug can't be underestimated. One bad batch and we have multiple fatalities. That's an outcome we can't afford to risk."

Maria strode out of the room, a five-foot-two firebrand, crooking her finger at Matt as she went.

He followed, pausing only to look back at Lara, question and something else, something serious, in his eyes. She nodded, that unspoken connection that always seemed to be there between them making a knot come to her throat.

They'd been partners a long time. The look on his usually calm, in-control face was not reassuring. This look said, we're in trouble.

Lara opened the front door of the station and pushed into the still-steaming late-afternoon sunlight. She dropped onto the low wall bordering the flower beds. Two days later, the bruises on her body from the explosion were brilliant purple and black, but the aches were finally beginning to fade. As were the memories of the explosion. What wasn't fading was the exhaustion. She and Matt had spent their off-time working the evidence from the fire and interviewing the neighbors on Billfish Drive. As far as she could tell, they'd gotten exactly nowhere.

She leaned her head against the brick wall behind her, letting the warmth soak into her back. Footsteps on the gravel parking lot to the side of their building jerked her to her feet.

A guy with a baby carrier rounded the corner toward her, a hunk of shaggy straight brown hair falling into his eyes. She relaxed slightly. Okay, so maybe she was still a little nervous.

"Oh, man. You look just like her. She said you did, but it's really…wow."

"What are you talking about?" She took a step back toward the building as the skinny guy—kid, really—came closer. He didn't look dangerous—just a guy in jeans and a polo shirt from some sandwich shop—but she felt like being extra cautious.

His eyes filled. "Emmy. You're Emmy's sister, aren't you?"

"What do you know about my sister?" Her voice came out harsh. She took a deep breath and gentled it. "I haven't heard from Emmy in more than a year. If you have, I'd like to know how she's doing."

The baby made a cranky sound and the young man shushed it, swaying the carrier. His eyes sheened with tears. "I haven't heard from her in three weeks. I think something may have happened to her."

When the baby started crying, he placed the carrier on the ground and unbuckled the straps, still shushing gently. He lifted a very young baby, maybe five months old, and tucked it into the crook of his arm.

"Look, I don't know how well you know my sister, but disappearing for three weeks is not exactly out of character for her." The baby found two of its fingers and began to suck, its eyes drifting closed and popping open as it fought sleep.

The young guy bounced the child back and forth. "That's the thing. It is out of character for her...now. She's been clean since she got pregnant. Maybe even before, and that's been, like, fourteen months. She's in school and she's a great mom."

Lara's chest seized up on her, like someone held it in a tight-fisted grip. She struggled to breathe normally.

The guy's tense shoulders relaxed as the baby

went to sleep, the tiny hand dropping to its side. "If you're Lara, this little darlin' would be your niece and I'm Ben, your brother-in-law. I found a newspaper article in Emmy's desk with your name circled and the station was listed. I thought it was worth a shot. But you haven't heard from her?"

She slowly shook her head and reached a trembling finger out to her niece's foot. Pink and perfect, the toes curled under when Lara ran her finger up the puckered baby skin. "She's beautiful."

"Her name is Charis. It means *grace*."

Ben seemed earnest and good-hearted. *Young.* And genuinely concerned for her sister. "So, she's married? To you?"

He smiled. A sweet, artless smile. "Yeah. I was surprised, too. She's pretty great."

For the first time in her life, Lara found herself envying her sister, what her sister had found with this young man who obviously loved her.

But nineteen-year-old Emmy was still missing. Lara forced herself past the revelations and into the present moment. "Was anything bothering Emmy? Anything that would have made her vulnerable?"

Thinking the worst seemed wrong, especially after meeting Ben and hearing that Emmy had changed. But she'd lived with drug and alcohol abuse her whole life, so she knew that all it took was a stressor and access.

Ben shook his head but then stopped. "Maybe. She was taking exams at the college in Fort Walton Beach right before she disappeared. I guess if someone asked, she might've been tempted. There was this study group she was in. Maybe one of them?"

"I'll see what I can find out. In the meantime, if you hear from her, do everything you can to find out where she is. It could mean her life." The worry for Emmy that was a constant presence had taken on a new urgency. This new drug out there was claiming victims. No one would be immune. And the people buying it wouldn't care what it could do to them, only what it would do for them. *Oh, Emmy.*

"I looked in all the old places she used to go. I didn't know where else to turn. Thank you." When she nodded, he pulled a piece of paper out of his pocket. "I've got to get the baby to day care and go to work, but here's my number. Please call me if you find anything. Anything at all."

He picked up the baby carrier and started for the parking lot, turning back only for one last long look before disappearing around the corner.

Lara's shoulders slumped. She had to go in and tell them she needed to leave, but she didn't even know where to start looking. Ben said he'd already looked in all of Emmy's old places. Lara hadn't seen Emmy in so long, there were probably a dozen new places that she wouldn't know about.

Turning toward the firehouse, she reached for the door handle and found Matt's broad chest instead. He'd obviously been standing there a while.

She closed her eyes. This day really couldn't get any worse.

"I've got to go." She angled away from him toward the parking lot and her car.

"Our shift ends in thirty minutes and we'll both go." He hadn't moved from his position by the front door, his arms crossed, his eyes hidden behind dark Ray-Bans.

"I don't want help."

"Do you even know where to start looking?"

Lara lifted a shoulder under her blue uniform shirt. "I'll figure it out. I always do."

"Fine." He jerked a nod.

"I can wait until shift ends." Her mind raced.

What was going on behind those sunglasses? She couldn't see his eyes, couldn't see what he was thinking. What if he was disappointed?

"Why didn't you tell me, Lara? Did you think I'd judge you?" His voice was lazy, but with all the time she'd spent as his partner, she knew he was ticked.

Sitting back down on the low wall that bordered their flower beds, she looked up at him. "No. I didn't."

At his snort, she raised her hands, classic defensive posture. *She* even knew it. "I really didn't, Matt. I've been defined my whole life by other people's actions. And for once, I just wanted to be me, on my own, no family giving everyone a reason to doubt me—or feel sorry for me."

He dropped his arms and came to sit by her on the wall, stretching his legs out in front of him, picking a weed out of the flower bed and throwing it onto the ground. "I can understand that."

Matt's dad was the Emerald County sheriff. He had a mom who not only knew how to cook, she *did* cook, and he and his two brothers were all superhero material from what she'd heard.

She stared at him. His eyes were on a beetle crawling on the sidewalk. When he glanced up there was something, some sadness she couldn't quite quantify in his expression, but when she looked again, he smiled and whatever it was had disappeared.

"This really isn't about us, is it?" His voice had gone husky.

When she slowly shook her head, he reached for her hand, gently squeezing her chilled fingers in his. "I know someone who might be able to help us if we run out of options. Do you have a picture of Emmy?"

"Not a recent one. But she looks just like me."

"I don't think it's a good idea to take you where I'd need to go." He stood, dusted the sand off his navy blue work pants and, as he walked away, she had to hurry to catch up with him.

She grabbed his arm. "Matt, you have to. This is only your business if I let it be."

"Trust me with your life but not your secrets. Isn't that how it's always worked, Lara?"

The words were sharp enough. She stopped.

Her heart ached. It wasn't that she didn't want to let Matt in. She did, sort of. But she'd learned at an early age that letting people "help" only led to more disappointment in the long run. That hard armor she'd built up was hard to shed. Even for Matt.

Something he couldn't possibly understand.

He pulled his sunglasses off, apology in his dark eyes. He reached for her, but this time she shrugged away from him.

Ten minutes. She had to get through ten more minutes of her shift and then she could go. With Matt or without him, she would find her sister.

The tones sounded. In unison, she and Matt turned and ran for the bay that housed the trucks. Her stomach sank as the voice over the loudspeaker announced a medical emergency. She knew that it would be a lot more than ten minutes before she went to look for Emmy.

The ambulance peeled out ahead of them, siren wailing. Lara stuffed her arms into her coat, grabbed her helmet and jumped onto the fire truck. She settled into the seat beside Matt, sliding on the leather as Santos laid on the horn before pulling into traffic.

Every run had the potential to be catastrophic for someone. Her heart beat faster. Her mind narrowed to one single goal, getting to the situation and making a difference. Her job—but also her calling.

She glanced at Matt. And saw deep worry lines instead of his typical grin.

She grabbed his arm. "Hey, what is it?"

He didn't hesitate, didn't try to sugarcoat. He lifted his walkie-talkie. "I just heard. The victim is female. Overdose."

FOUR

The young woman on the ground didn't move as paramedic Daniel Hudson tried to find an airway. She was in bad shape. And despite the blond hair, she also obviously wasn't Lara's sister. The girl was still wearing her sweater with the private school insignia.

Matt tried to get the attention of the girl's friend, the only one who had stuck around to wait for help. He touched the kid's arm with a gloved hand. "Can you tell me what she took?"

The guy bounced on his feet, looking frantically from Dumpster to pile of trash bags in the alleyway, refusing to meet Matt's eyes. "She didn't take anything, I swear. She just fell down and started having some kind of fit, shaking and stuff comin' out of her mouth. I thought she was gonna die."

Matt saw Lara turn toward Daniel and knew

she would relay the new information about the seizure to the paramedic.

Tears gathered in the kid's eyes. Looking about twelve in his own high school uniform polo, he glanced around again and poised on his toes like he was about to take off.

Matt grabbed his arm. "Hey, listen, you did the right thing. You called us and you're giving her a chance, the only one she's got."

The guy bounced back toward Matt. "I gotta go. I can't hang around here. You gotta let me go, man."

Matt shot a look back toward Daniel, where he was intubating the girl on the ground. Not a good sign. "I need to know what kind of drugs she was doing. If she took something that made her sick, it may have the same effect on other people. If you took the same drug, it may make you sick, too."

The guy shrank back. "I don't do drugs."

"Right." He was still holding the boy's wrist, could feel the blood catapulting through his veins. The kid was scared, but... "Pretty fast pulse for someone who doesn't take drugs. Come on, what's your name?"

The kid swallowed hard, his Adam's apple bobbing. "Will."

"And your friend?"

"Kristin." The teenager's voice shook.

"All right, Will. Listen, dude, you may be the only one that can help Kristin. Look at my uniform. I'm not the cops, I'm not interested in what you did that was against the law."

The prep school kid eased his heels to the ground, relaxing slightly. "It was some new stuff. An orange powder, the guy called it Bright Orange, but it looked sort of like an orange drink mix."

"Did Kristin do more than you?"

Misery was written all over Will's face, shone in the weepy blue eyes. Matt felt for him but couldn't give in, not on something so important. "Will?"

"No. She shoots up. I don't." Beads of sweat popped on Will's forehead.

Behind them, Matt heard a shout and turned toward it. Lara held the IV while Todd bagged the teenager. Daniel raised the gurney and moved her quickly to the bus. In this situation it was pack and go. They didn't have time to stabilize her at the scene.

Will started to cry in earnest. "Oh, man. Her mom is gonna freak."

"Give me a number to call."

The boy wiped his nose on his sleeve. "I can't. I promised Kristin I wouldn't ever tell."

"Will, no matter what you do or don't do, her mother is going to find out about this. Give me a number, please."

The kid mumbled it under his breath, but Matt caught it anyway, punching it into his phone for when they knew more.

Daniel looked back and caught Matt's eye, shaking his head. He had his fingers in the cleft of the girl's neck, searching for a pulse and, by the expression on his face, not finding one. He began chest compressions as Lara slammed the bay doors and banged on them so Todd would know it was safe to take off.

Matt took a few steps back, silently guiding Will farther away from the scene. "I know it's hard to answer questions when your friend is in such bad shape, but this is the best way you can help her, I promise."

Will's body shuddered involuntarily, the high of the drug burned up in the adrenaline dumped in his system when Kristin began to seize.

Matt reached for the boy's arm. His skin was cold and clammy. He needed to be seen at the hospital, too. "Let me call your parents, Will."

"No!"

"It's either me or the cops over there, but one way or another, your parents are going to find out. I'll make sure they know you did the right thing for Kristin."

Slumping to sit on the curb, Will mumbled a second number as the ambulance pulled away with his friend inside. A friend that most likely would not survive the ride to the hospital. The siren began its slow wail.

Matt made the call to Will's mother, stressing that he would be fine but that she needed to get down there as soon as possible.

Lara stripped off latex gloves as she walked up. "How's it going?"

"I talked to Will's mother. She should be here in a couple of minutes. Can you keep an eye on him while I watch for her? I'd like to talk to her about an E.R. visit before she sees him."

Lara crouched down beside Will. "Hey, how are you feeling?"

"All right, I guess." The kid's eyes didn't focus on hers. Matt was right. He needed to be evaluated. "Is Kristin going to be okay?"

"I'm gonna be straight with you. She wasn't breathing when we got here and it doesn't look good for her." Kicking aside a squashed beer can, Lara eased to the curb to sit beside him. She pulled a blood-pressure cuff out of the emergency kit the paramedics had left behind.

Will pressed the heels of his hands hard

against his eyes, like maybe he could remove the memory of all that had happened this afternoon if he pressed hard enough. Sound escaped— words, but so disturbed she couldn't make them out.

She eased his arm out, wrapped the cuff around it and put the stethoscope in the bend of his elbow. "What did you say?"

"I should've stopped her. I should've said no. This wouldn't have happened." He looked up at the sun-streaked sky, just deepening into twilight. Lara pumped the blood-pressure cuff and listened. When she had the reading she held his arm.

"Look at me." She waited for his red, swollen eyes to meet hers. "You didn't cause this. Kristin chose to take the drugs. She's responsible for that choice. Just like you're responsible for yours."

"I don't want to take them anymore." He gripped her arm, his fingers frantic.

"You don't have to. You can get help. All you have to do is ask for it." Lara winged a prayer that he would ask for help. And that God would be there to guide him when he did.

Will couldn't meet her eyes, his head dropping to his knees, his voice an anguished whisper. *"How?"*

"The first thing you need to do is tell your mom. Right when she gets here." Lara could well imagine what his mom would feel.

"Tell your mom what?" A woman stood behind them, her tennis skirt and short pony-tail wisping in the breeze. She looked like the epitome of a country-club mother.

"Mom?" When he caught sight of her, Will jumped to his feet, his nose beginning to run again. He gulped air in great sobs.

His mother wrapped her arms around him, even though he towered over her by at least five inches. Emotion warred on her face between anger and frustration, relief, shock. Yeah, definitely shock.

She pushed him away from her gently. "What do you need to tell me, Will?"

He hesitated, and the mother in her started to reach for him again but instead she caught Matt's eye. She took a deep breath. "I need to hear you say it."

"I'm...I'm in trouble, Mom, and I need your help." He sniffed once and then again as he swiped his sleeve across his face. "Please?"

"Will, what were you *thinking?*" His mother's voice climbed.

Lara opened her mouth, like she was about to say something, probably about how much luckier this mom was than the mom of the kid in the ambulance. Matt put a hand on her arm. She pressed her lips together.

Will's mom took a deep, calming breath. "You know what, it doesn't matter. I'm going to do whatever it takes to help you get better. Okay?"

His heart in his eyes, the kid nodded. He looked around at the alley where they stood, the trash stacked against the wall, crumpled beer cans and cigarette butts littering the ground. "I don't want to spend the rest of my life like this."

With his mom's arm around him, he turned back to Matt. "Now what?"

"Now you go to the hospital to get checked out. We can take you in an ambulance or your mom can drive you." Matt's coffee-brown eyes were reassuring, his confident manner giving the boy a reason to believe him. He handed Will a Gatorade from the gas station across the street. "Make sure you drink all of this. Okay?"

Will nodded, his restless fingers cracking the cap before he asked the next question. "What about, you know, them?" He motioned to the cops waiting a dozen feet away.

Matt looked at the police. "The drug you took is dangerous and we want it off our streets. We'll have more questions for you, bud, but right now the first priority is keeping you alive."

Will's mom pulled her son close. "Thank you."

Lara nodded. "Be prepared for a long road. Don't give up."

Matt waved J.T. over with two fingers and had the kid's mom sign off that she was transporting him to the hospital herself. As the mother and son walked toward their BMW, Matt turned to Lara. "Were you talking to Will or his mom? When you said there'd be a long road."

"Either. Both." She shook her head. "It's going to be just as hard for her as it is for him. Maybe harder. But maybe he'll have a chance, seeing firsthand exactly what the consequences can be."

Matt touched her hand. "We'll find her, Lara."

The memory of Kristin, the young girl they'd just transported, flashed in Lara's mind. How many times had Lara saved her sister, found her in situations that were so similar to the one today? How many more could Emmy survive before she ended up like that prep school kid, barely clinging to life?

"We're off tomorrow. We can spend all day looking." Santos and J.T. had finished cleaning up the scene, tossing the paper wrappers and syringe covers, so Matt walked toward the rig for the ride back to the station.

"I can't wait until tomorrow, Matt." As the truck pulled away from the scene, Lara looked at the place where the teenager had fallen from an overdose. "It's too dangerous."

"It's too dangerous to go to those places at night. Get a night's rest. Tomorrow we'll find her."

She shook her head. Sleep wouldn't come easy tonight, knowing this potent new drug was out there. She may as well be looking for Emmy.

"What about your mom? What will you tell her when you go out tonight?"

Lara looked out the window at the street passing by. Her sister could be in any one of those houses and Lara would never know it. If she could, she would knock on every door, ask every person.

Honestly, she didn't even know where to start. She glanced at Matt as Santos pulled the truck into the station and parked. He'd been a lot of things to her since they'd started working together. Coworker, partner...friend. It was time that she started treating him like one. Trusting him to be one.

Matt swung off the rig onto the concrete floor of the truck bay. "I'll pick you up at eight in the morning. We'll look for her all day."

"What about the case?"

He shrugged. "What about it?"

"I don't want to take you away from the work you need to be doing."

"Lara. I saw your face when you were packing that girl for transport. She could *be* your sister. Finding Emmy is important. And while we're looking for her, we'll also be looking for links to our explosion the other day. Okay?" He hung his turnout coat on his hook and stepped out of his Nomex pants, leaving them on the floor for their next call-out.

"Okay." Lara shrugged out of her coat as he walked away, reaching into his uniform pocket for his car keys. "Hey, Matt."

He turned back.

"Don't be late."

He laughed as he walked out the open door of the bay toward the parking lot.

"Hey, Matt." He turned back to her again, his dark brown eyes soft, a hint of amusement playing around his mouth.

"Thanks."

He nodded once and disappeared around the corner.

* * *

The next afternoon, Matt pulled the car up to a two-story stucco mansion in a golf-course community known for its upscale homes. Lara was curious, but the stony look on his normally agreeable face stopped her questions. They'd already checked half a dozen areas that they knew were drug hangouts from previous calls, but none of the people loitering around them had remembered seeing anyone fitting Emmy's description.

"Matt, who lives here?" The sluggish breeze rattled the fronds of the palm trees lining the drive.

"Just this guy I know. I'd tell you to stay in the car, but it's probably safer with me. Don't wander off, okay? And don't say anything to him. Promise me."

She swallowed the questions back. "I promise."

Matt strode up the walk onto the huge columned porch and rang the doorbell. A gigantic overmuscled man in a black suit opened the door and stared at them as if daring them to enter. The telltale bulge under the arm of his coat told her that he was prepared to stop them if they tried.

Matt held his hands open, arms away from

his sides. "I'm looking for Baby J. Tell him Matt Clark is here."

The big dude looked Matt over from top to bottom, totally ignoring Lara. "Why should I?"

"Because Baby J would want you to." He stared into the man's eyes. Lara's chest quaked. Give her a burning building any day.

"Wait here."

Lara grabbed Matt's arm. "What is this place? What's a guy named Baby J doing in this neighborhood?"

"I'll explain everything later. Right now we just need to concentrate on getting out of here alive."

The door cracked open and the huge guy motioned them into the entry hall. Lara followed Matt, stepping onto the Italian marble floor. She looked up two floors to a fresco on the ceiling. Wow.

"Spread 'em." The bodyguard wasn't amused. He patted Matt down from armpits to ankles and turned to Lara.

Matt put a hand on the big guy's chest before he could touch her. "Is this absolutely necessary?"

The huge man crossed his arms and stared at Matt. "She gets frisked or she waits outside."

"Matt, it's fine." She gritted her teeth as the bodyguard ran his hands loosely over her body.

The enormous man motioned them into the living room and took a position just inside the front door. Seconds later, a guy came into the room—a guy who looked like a college student, in khakis and a button-down oxford shirt.

"Matt." He walked toward Matt with both hands held out and gave him a brother-to-brother kind of hug. "What are you doing here? This isn't your scene." He hesitated, narrowed his eyes. "You're not looking to score, are you?"

Just like that, it became crystal clear to Lara. This guy, who would've fit in at any college in the nation, was a drug dealer. And Matt knew him personally.

"No, J, I'm not looking to score."

Baby J shook his head, flipping frat-boy bangs back in place. "That's a relief. I wasn't going to enjoy telling you no."

A hint of a smile pulled at the corner of Matt's mouth. "I'm here for information."

The affable face faded. "I heard you were a cop or something like that."

"Something like that." Matt crossed his arms,

his own muscles bulging against his plain black T-shirt.

"I'm no narc, Matt. Not even for you." Baby J leaned against a brick wall weathered to look like an Italian villa. He shot a glance at his bodyguard.

"I'm not asking you to be. My friend here is missing her sister. The girl's been into drugs before and we think she may be again. Listen, J, I don't know who her supplier is and don't care, I'm just hoping you might've seen her."

Baby J looked Lara over. "She look like you?"

"Yes." She swallowed hard, remembering Matt's admonishment not to talk.

J hesitated, pursed his lips, continuing to stare at Lara. A cool chill settled in her stomach, but she looked into his bright blue eyes.

Still staring at Lara, he said, "There's a shooting gallery on 22nd Street where some hard users hang. That's not my kind of clientele, but paths cross occasionally. I heard a guy they call Reefer talking about someone that could be your sister. She may not be there now."

Matt stepped closer to Lara. "She could be. We'll check it out."

Baby J pulled a slim case out of his pocket and handed Matt a card. On the card, the text simply said J and a cell-phone number. "That should get you a pass in. If you get in any trouble, you call that number. I should be able to pull some strings."

Who were these people? And how did Matt fit into this crowd?

Matt nodded and turned toward the door and, as the bodyguard opened it for them, even started to follow her out. Instead he stopped and turned back to the drug dealer. "I figure this makes us even. Thanks."

A small smile flitted across J's face as he slowly shook his head. "You saved my brother's life. We'll never be even."

FIVE

Matt pulled away from the curb in J's fancy neighborhood, his fingers clenched around the steering wheel. He'd seen the look on Lara's face when she'd realized just exactly who J was.

"So, do you want to tell me how you met him?" Her voice was soft. He looked at her and she glanced away, brushing her bangs out of her eyes.

He lifted a shoulder, uncomfortable. "It was a couple of years ago. I just happened to answer the call when his brother was shot."

"Right. How many other people took that call?"

That night really wasn't a memory Matt wanted to dredge up. He'd treated the kid, the kid made it. It's what they did. No more. "I haven't seen him since then, but J sent me a message through the E.R. staff that if I ever needed anything to let him know. Today we needed something that I thought he could help with."

"He doesn't look like a user." He looked like a fraternity brother.

"He's not. He's too smart for that. He knows better than to get his head messed up by the drugs, but don't be fooled by his looks, Lara. J is not a nice guy. He's a businessman. And his business is as rough as it gets."

"I know, but thanks." She pointed. "That next turn is 22nd Street. It curves down along the water, but it's pretty scary in there. We took a call down that street last fall."

The wheels crunched on fallen leaves and debris. The houses at the end of the street had been damaged in the hurricanes of the past, and the owners had obviously chosen to take their insurance payment rather than clean up and rebuild.

Those people looking for a place to hide, crash or escape had built their own little community here. And those who would take advantage of them had invaded this property, too.

Matt had never wanted to carry a gun. He'd been raised around them and had known how to shoot even as a kid. But he'd never wished for one or thought that he'd needed one for his own protection. Until now.

He'd been licensed and certified at the Florida Department of Law Enforcement in preparation for his new job. And as a cop, he'd carry his service weapon.

But just like he'd known better than to carry his sidearm into Baby J's backyard, a handgun found on him here would only escalate things. And J's business card, well, that was as much of a weapon as any gun he could carry.

Matt switched off the ignition and turned to Lara. "Stay close. This is not going to be pretty. You know that, right?"

"I know. I'll be fine. This isn't my first crack house, Matt."

"It's your first one like this." Matt opened the door and stepped out. The decaying underbrush seemed to underscore the rotting buildings. What used to be the driveway had been reclaimed by the surrounding forest, with limbs and vines battling with moss to gain control.

Two young women were lounging behind the ruined house, but they barely looked up when Matt and Lara walked up. One of them raised a hand and let it flop back to her lap. Their eyes were hollow, deep circles marring their complexions, their clothes dirty. The overwhelming desire for the next hit obviously outweighed the need for food, family, health.

It was so incredibly sad. The futility of it all made Matt sick at his stomach. The door barely hung on the hinges, but he reached for the handle anyway. Lara hesitated, her eyes focused on one of the women in the chairs.

"Matt, that girl needs fluids. She's dehydrated. Did you see her lips?"

He pulled her to the side of the door. "I know it's hard, but you can't interfere now, not if you want to find Emmy. Later, we'll see if there's something we can do."

Lara looked back at the girls—and that was what they were, just two girls, barely out of high school. Matt could easily see the battle she was waging in her mind, and why not? He felt the same himself. It went against everything they did, everything they *were,* to see a person in need and pass by. It made no difference that these people had chosen their path. They were lost now.

And for Lara it would be so much worse because in every young woman she met, she would see her sister. "Honey, listen, if you can't do this, I can go in by myself."

Lara lifted her hands to her face, scrubbing them across the surface. When she opened her eyes, they were clear. "I'm fine. I'll be *fine.*"

She pushed the door open and walked through

it. Matt followed close behind. Even basic necessities like plumbing and electricity were missing here. Those had been destroyed in the hurricane and never repaired, and although the windows were mostly broken out, the stench inside the oppressive humidity of the place rolled over him. His stomach heaved. He held his breath.

People were everywhere. On sagging couches, lying in blankets. In the corner, a young woman lounged in a chair. At her feet on the dirty floor was an infant, about nine months old, chewing on a saltine cracker.

Beside him, he heard Lara whisper, "Dear God."

His hands itched to grab the baby and run. He clenched his fists. "Look around, see if you see her. Let's start upstairs, but be careful."

The stairs were still fairly intact, with only the bottom few rotting through. At the top of the stairs were old bedrooms, still with the same furniture the original owners had left here. Matt motioned Lara to take the one on the right and he took the room on the left. Like downstairs, people were in every nook and cranny. In the bathroom, Matt opened the shower door to find a man curled around his pipe asleep, but no sign of Emmy.

People barely raised their heads, apparently past feeling curiosity or even reaction.

He met Lara back in the hall. "Anything?"

She shook her head, her hazel eyes big and haunted, her breath coming in short, sharp puffs. "I thought what we saw in town was bad. This beats it all, beats anything I've ever seen before."

"I know." In the humidity, her hair had curled and stuck damp ringlets to her cheek and neck. He brushed it away from her face and for once she didn't step away. "Let's check the bedrooms downstairs and then get out of here."

One of the bedrooms had a tree growing through the wall. The other one was occupied, but neither one of the women looked anything like Lara. Back in the living room, the mother of the little baby gave them a curious stare, the first sign of awareness he'd seen.

Matt walked over to her, then stooped down so he could look at the baby's eyes, check for dehydration. "I'm looking for a girl who could be in trouble. Do you think you can help?"

The woman reached for the baby and pulled him onto her lap. "You're gonna have to give me more to go on that that. Ain't nobody in here that doesn't match that description."

Matt forced a chuckle when it didn't feel

anything like funny. "She looks like my friend over there. Blond hair, greenish eyes."

The woman squinted her eyes trying to get a better look at Lara. "She looks kinda familiar, but I don't know."

The back door slammed open. A big dude with a T-shirt loose over his jeans stepped into the room. The dealer, most likely. Or his enforcer. And yeah, that could be a gun under his shirt.

Matt reached a hand out to Lara. "Time to go."

She gripped his hand and walked with him to the door, right past the enormous man standing with his arms crossed by their only escape route.

He didn't say anything or try to stop Lara, but as Matt passed, the dealer stared Matt down and lifted his shirt to show him the handgun wedged into the waistband of his jeans.

Matt raised his hands as he edged past. "We were just leaving."

The man stepped aside to let them pass, but as they walked out the door, Matt could feel the guy's eyes boring into his back. At every level, this business was scary. It would be so easy for people to fall in and not be able to see a way out.

The two women who'd been out there before had disappeared. Lara's shoulders slumped.

Matt gripped her hand tighter. "We'll find Emmy. Don't give up."

She took three slow steps toward the car. "I'm not, it's just so horrible. It wouldn't have surprised me to find Emmy there. She can't seem to stay away. *Why?* I mean, she has this great guy that loves her? And that beautiful baby?"

Matt blinked. He knew from personal experience that having it all wasn't the answer. "Sometimes it's not that simple."

She smacked the window of the car with her hand. And it must have made her feel a little better because she did it again.

Matt beeped the lock and opened the door for Lara.

"I'm so scared for her." Lara's nose got red as she swallowed back tears. She let out a half laugh as Matt slid into the driver's seat beside her. "And at the same time I want to kill her. It makes no sense."

"It makes perfect sense. She's your baby sister."

"Yeah. And something tells me she's really in trouble. Those people, Matt." She twisted her fingers in her lap, uncharacteristic of his in-charge, independent friend and partner. "I don't know what to do next."

"We get something to eat, regroup and start again." Power of positive thinking, right? Lara needed a boost of encouragement even though finding her sister alive wasn't exactly a sure thing at this point. And God help them all if she wasn't. "We also need to go back over the case evidence piece by piece. I don't think anyone at that place knew anything about the drug we're trying to find. I got a good look at some of what they were holding. It looked like crystal meth, not a drink powder."

Lara took a deep breath, squared her shoulders. "Okay. I think we should go back to the scene of the blast, talk to the neighbors again. Maybe there's something we missed." As they pulled out of the tangle of underbrush onto the main road, the trees opened up and blue sky appeared.

"And Emmy?"

"We're out of options. I need to check the hospitals." Her eyes suddenly full, she turned away, toward the window. Matt sent a silent prayer heavenward that she would be able to find some peace.

He reached for her hand, the other on her head. When she didn't pull away, he didn't know if it was a victory or surrender. "There's one more place we should probably call."

She didn't turn around.

"I know. I don't even want to think it. But I have to—I have to call the morgue."

Lara sat on the hood of Matt's Charger with her cell phone, making calls that no one should have to make. *Have you admitted a patient named Emmy Hughes? Emmy Payne? Any unidentified patients? She has blond hair and hazel eyes.*

She closed the phone and rubbed her eyes, letting the warmth of the car soak into her bones. She wanted to find Emmy and shake her until her teeth fell out. And she wanted to grab her and hold her close like she used to when Emmy was a little girl. They'd been through so much, the two of them.

Matt leaned against the fence across the street talking to the neighbor. The burned-out shell of the lab that had exploded loomed next to them, a reminder of just how fast things could go south.

One more call. The one that she'd been avoiding thinking about all afternoon. She forced herself to press the numbers she'd gotten from information and waited.

"Emerald County coroner's office."

Lara's throat closed up on her.

"Hello?"

She swallowed hard, forcing herself to push words out. "I'm calling about my sister."

"I'm sorry, can you speak up a little?" The voice on the other end of the line sounded kind, if a little frustrated.

Lara cleared her throat and tried again. "My sister is missing and I'm calling to see if she's been brought in. Her name is Emmy Hughes Payne. She has blond hair and hazel eyes."

"Let me check our log and I'll get right back to you." Soft music began to play in Lara's ear, probably meant to be soothing, but it just set her nerves on edge.

A click and the voice came back. "Hon, we haven't had anyone by that name or with that description. I'm sorry I couldn't help you."

"I'm not." The news sent relief flooding through her, despite the fact that they still hadn't a clue where to search for Emmy. "Thank you for looking."

Matt shook hands with the neighbor, taking his time walking across the street to the car. His warm brown eyes held the question he didn't ask. She gave him thumbs-up and when his shoulders relaxed in relief, she smiled. He'd been more than a partner through this, he'd been a friend.

She shouldn't have expected any less. He was a good guy.

"No news is good news?" He slid onto the hood of the car beside her.

"At this point I'll take it. What about you? Did you learn anything new?"

"Corroboration on our person of interest." Matt stared at the burned shell of a house. "I showed him the sketch. He ID'd the drawing as the person who lived here, said he'd seen him around."

"Did you get a name?" One break. Come on. A name.

"Not really. He said the guy's name was Al, but he doesn't know the last name. He remembers hearing car doors a lot at night, but just figured the guy for a party animal."

"It might take a while to go through the database, but if we have a name and know what kind of car he drives, we might be able to find him using DMV photos."

"Al could be Albert." Matt slid his notebook from his back pocket and started jotting the names.

"Allen."

Matt wrote it down. "Alfred."

"Al…istair." She bit her lip when Matt started to write it, then looked up with a quizzical look—*how do you spell that*—and she started to laugh. "You never know."

"I'll call Maria and get her tech team on this." He looked down the nearly empty street. "You know, you'd figure in a neighborhood like this that there'd be at least one granny keeping watch, but most of the people on this street are working couples, no kids."

"If that's a choice our unsubs made, maybe it's an identifier we can use to find their next place. I'd guess that if they laid enough groundwork to set up a lab like that here, they wouldn't want to move on unless they absolutely had to." She jumped off the car. "Come on. I say we pick up a pizza and work our way through the foreclosure list. We can at least narrow it down to a few places to check out tomorrow."

Matt didn't move, just sat studying her. Self-conscious, she smoothed her T-shirt, fought the urge to look behind her. *"What?"*

"Don't take this the wrong way, okay?"

He was scaring her a little. Lara put one hand on her hip. "Dude, seriously, spit it out."

He kicked at a pebble on the asphalt street. So not a Matt move that she took a step closer.

"You're so smart and you don't give yourself nearly enough credit."

She could feel the flush begin at the base of her neck. "Well, that does it. I'm gonna have to hit you now." When he jerked his head up, she held up her hands. "*Kidding*—can we eat now?"

He laughed, and there was the easygoing guy she knew. "Okay, changing the subject. I'm pretty sure there's a pizza calling my name." He climbed into the car. "Coming?"

"Yes, I'm coming. Do you really think I'd let you get pizza without me?" They'd been friends and because of her fear they'd almost lost it. She was so grateful that they hadn't. Matt was too important to her to lose. That thought in itself should've scared her but it didn't. It made her feel special.

Like she hadn't felt in a long time. Maybe ever.

Lara flipped open another of the files spread out on the table in front of her. On-duty hours had three speeds: bored, asleep or screaming activity. Fortunately the boredom gave her time to comb through the files. Again.

She dug her hand into the open box of sugary cereal and tossed a few into her mouth. She and

Matt had spent hours last night going through the foreclosure list, typing the addresses into a search engine and looking at the bird's-eye satellite pictures on the off chance that some evidence of drug cooking could be seen in the photos. Nothing. At least nothing current enough to help. The police investigators on the task force would have to physically check every house on the list.

As far as the evidence from the fire scene, she and Matt had reached a dead end there, too. The materials they'd been able to identify had either been paid for in cash—like the propane tanks—or stripped of identifiers. According to Maria Fuentes, there was no physical evidence to lead them to any one person. There was plenty of DNA on the drug paraphernalia left in the salvageable rooms at the site of the explosion that they could nail the losers with once they caught them.

These criminals, whoever they were, were smart. Whatever they learned now would be the result of Matt's continued interviews with the neighbors or, possibly, new information about the drug as it spread in their community.

But even then, like with the teenagers the other day, law enforcement wasn't always able to identify the source. And meanwhile, more and more people like her sister were at risk.

She laid her forehead on the table. It always came back to Emmy. They had to find these guys, whoever they were. Because everyone affected by this drug was someone's Emmy.

Frustrated, she sat up and shoved the files away, scattering pages.

Matt dropped into the chair beside her. "Not having a good morning?"

She sighed. "Just can't see us finding a way out of this anytime soon unless something breaks in the case. I want that to happen, but I'm afraid of it, too. Because it might mean someone else dying, like the teenager the other day."

"Everyone on this task force is doing everything in our power to make sure that's not going to happen." His voice was firm, the look in his eyes resolute. If she didn't already know it, it wouldn't be hard for him to convince her.

"I know. It just seems like it's taking forever."

J.T. chased Miguel Santos into the kitchen, brandishing a Ping-Pong paddle. "Give me the ball."

"No way, man. You are driving me crazy with that thing." Miguel faced off against J.T. on the opposite side of the kitchen table.

"I'm playing with it."

Santos tucked the ball under his arm. "You've been bouncing it off that paddle for the last forty-five minutes. I'll tell you what I'm going to do with it if you don't quit."

"Oooooh, big talk, short man." J.T. bowed up at Santos.

Matt held out his hand. "Give me the ball."

"No way." Both men turned on him at the same moment.

"Come on. We'll all play a game. Truth-or-dare pong. Unless you're too scared." Matt held out his hand again, his eyes already daring them, daring them to back down.

J.T. looked around at each person speculatively. "Okay. I'll take you on."

Matt took a glass tumbler from the cabinet and put it in the middle of the table. "Rules are as follows. You can't lean over. The ball can only take one bounce, but it has to take at least one bounce. You only get one try."

Santos cleared his throat. "J.T."

"What?" J.T. looked at Lara, his sandy-reddish hair standing on end. *"What?"*

"Nothing, J.T. Carry on, Matt." She was going to enjoy watching this.

"You have to follow through on the truth or dare. No backing out."

J.T. snorted. "As if."

"Final rule. Ladies first." Matt's white-hot grin split his face as he held the ball out to her.

Oh, yeah, she was really going to enjoy *watching.* Fine.

She took the ball out of Matt's hand. The key was not thinking about it too much. She took aim and bounced it off the table right into the cup.

Santos hooted. "Whoa. Now you call who goes next."

"Go for it." Lara elbowed J.T. on her right.

J.T. tried several different body positions before taking careful aim and bouncing the ball. It missed and bounced into the spaghetti pot bubbling on the stove.

"Nice one, J.T." Matt poked him. "Okay, Lara, he's all yours."

"Truth or dare, J.T.?" She tilted her head waiting for his answer.

He narrowed his eyes. "Truth."

Oh, man. She hadn't been expecting that. "Okay, what's the thing in your life that you most regret?"

He made a show of thinking about it while he washed the red sauce off of the ball. "Okay, I got it. Not kissing Miss Mulholland, my second-grade teacher, when I had the chance."

"Come on. A real one." Santos walked to the stove and stirred the sauce, tasted it with the end of the wooden spoon, mulled it over a second and added some more oregano.

J.T. looked hurt, but then he shrugged. "Okay, I was just joking about Miss Mulholland, even though she was really hot."

"J.T." Lara laughed. "Come on."

"There was this girl in one of my classes in college. I wanted to ask her out. We never talked, but she was always looking at me and smiling. I finally got up the nerve to ask her out. She told me she'd just started dating this other guy, but if I had asked her a week earlier she would've loved to. I found out later they got married." He stuck his fingers through his hair, making it stand up even more. "I always wondered, what if?"

Santos sniffed back a fake tear. "That's so touching. Okay, pick someone."

"Definitely you, hotshot. Go for it." J.T. lounged back in one of the kitchen chairs, his legs sprawled out in front of him.

"You just have to have the right technique." Santos acted like he was about to take a free throw and tossed the ball, which bounced over the cup.

J.T. shot to his feet. "Truth or dare, lose-ah?"

"Dare." Santos crossed his muscular arms, like, *come on, take your best shot.*

"Eat one of those habañeros you're always putting in the food. With no water." J.T. stared into Santos's face, daring him to back out.

"That's a sucker dare. Hand them over." Santos took the jar from J.T. and popped one of the peppers into his mouth. He chewed. His eyes watered and his nose started to run. When his face turned red, Lara edged toward the door, ready to call Daniel and Todd for emergency treatment.

Santos finally swallowed. He opened his mouth to show J.T. he'd done it. "Ha."

"Okay, eww." Lara put her hand up. "Enough of that. Pick someone, Santos."

"Matteo, you go."

Matt took the laissez-faire approach, tossed the ball without really thinking about it and made it. "Skills, gentlemen. Okay, Lara, I liked your style last time. Let's see you do it again."

Her strategy worked last time, so she took aim and tossed the ball. It hit the table, hit the rim of the glass and bounced off. Santos hooted again.

She met each one of their eyes with a deadly stare. "Do your worst. Dare me."

J.T. whispered in Santos's ear. Santos belly laughed and whispered back. Matt looked at her and shrugged.

Finally, J.T. said, "Here's your dare. You go out on a date with Matt."

Matt went deadly still.

"That's the worst you could come up with?" She forced herself to laugh, but the ache in the center of her chest made it nearly impossible. Without even knowing it, they'd hit on her most personal wish.

Santos butted in. "There's more. You have to text a picture, so we know you actually did it."

Matt stood up. "That's a little unfa—"

"Shut up, Matt. I've never backed down on a dare in my life. I'm not gonna start now." She picked the ball up off the floor and held it out. "J.T.?"

The alert tones sounded. The ball fell to the floor. Lara turned away from the table, not having to look to know that the others did the same. She turned the burner off on the spaghetti and put the lid on it as the dispatcher's voice announced a house fire at Square-Rigger Drive.

She ran for her gear, stepping into her pants and hiking them up. Sliding her arms into her coat, she grabbed her helmet and headed for the rig.

Paramedic Daniel Hudson and EMT Todd Blankenship pulled out first in the ambulance, siren wailing.

With Matt firing questions full speed into the walkie-talkie, Lara finished putting on her hood, strapping her coat closed around it. Something niggled at the back of her mind, bothering her.

"Hey." Matt pushed her arm to get her attention. "What's up?"

"Why?"

He leaned forward, almost yelling over the noise of the truck's engine. "You've got a weird look on your face. Listen, that date thing. You don't have to do it. We'll just take a picture and send it to those fools. They'll never have to know."

"It's not that." Although the fact that she'd agreed to go on a date with Matt was something she would have to think about later. Or maybe he didn't want to go out with her anymore. And that thought was a whole new thing to worry about.

"That blast have you screwed up in the head about going in?"

"No, it's not that, either." She frowned. Something about that address sounded familiar. "Wasn't that address on the list of foreclosures we looked at?"

Matt's eyes widened. "Yeah, maybe it was."

"Got smoke," J.T. called back from the front seat.

Santos pulled the rig to the curb. The crew bailed out, Matt shouting orders as they put their helmets on. "Lara and I are first in on the pipe. Santos, you and J.T. behind us on the door. We're pretty sure this house was on the foreclosure list like the lab that exploded, so keep your eyes open."

It wasn't their first call since the explosion, but it was their first fire. *Was* it messing with her head? She had a bad feeling about this. Starting with hearing the address, there'd been a knot in the pit of her stomach.

Prone more to practicality than flights of fancy, it wasn't like her. But she did not want to go in that building.

Matt had the ax in his hands, ready to knock through the front door locks. He jerked his head toward the porch and started toward the house. Lara followed.

It was a simple ranch-style house. The overgrown yard didn't look like it held any hidden dangers. The trash cans were around the side of the house, but she saw no empty antifreeze bottles or stained filters or anything that would suggest that the building was being used as a lab.

Matt pulled his SCBA mask down over his face and climbed the steps to the porch. "Come on, Hughes. It's only getting hotter in there."

She *wasn't* scared. That feeling in the pit of her stomach didn't mean she didn't have the guts to do this job.

"Okay, let's go." She pulled her mask down, settled her helmet and moved to her position beside Matt. As he pulled the ax back to slam the door, she caught sight of something that made her blood run cold, despite her heavy equipment. *"Stop!"*

SIX

Matt halted midmotion at Lara's yell. "What?"

"Look. Right there." She pointed but didn't touch, beads of sweat breaking out on her forehead.

A tiny wire, almost invisible, was barely noticeable in the crack of the door.

Matt muttered a prayer of thanks that she'd seen the wire, that he'd had the sense to listen to her and that they'd both walk away from this one. He turned to the crew. "Back away from the house. Put some water on it from the outside."

He jogged away from the door, pulling his mask off and talking into his walkie-talkie, calling for the bomb squad, every cop in the area and another fire station to be dispatched. Within seconds, he could hear more sirens in the distance.

His heart pounded. He stopped behind the

rig. He and Lara stood for a moment just staring at each other and then, because he needed to, he jerked Lara into his arms, knocking her helmet off in the process.

She went stiff in his embrace, but then she twisted his coat in her fists, pulling him closer. "You're okay. We're okay."

It had been a near thing. A very near thing. He could have lost her.

Just as fast, he let go, stepping back. "Sorry. I just…" Matt rubbed a hand across his face, stopping to look at it. "My hands are shaking."

Lara shot a look back at the house, flames now visible at the roof line, obviously giving him a second to get it together. "We need to get the area evacuated in case this place blows. There's no way of knowing what's in there."

Matt nodded, taking a deep breath. "Right. We need more water on the roof and Ladder 2 is on their way. Let's make sure the immediate neighbors are out of their homes and when the cops get here, we can have them evac the whole street."

"Got it." Lara stooped to pick up her helmet. "I'll get Todd and Daniel started on the west side."

"Hey, Bump."

She turned back to face him, her hair flying in the hot summer breeze.

"Nice catch."

She grinned. "Yeah, I saved your worthless hide."

He laughed as he raised the walkie-talkie to his lips again. "Dispatch, how far out is Ladder 2?"

The bomb squad would come, but they wouldn't be able to do anything. All any of them could do was control the blaze. Surround and drown. And for that, they needed more water.

Matt saw Todd cross the street to start knocking on doors as the bomb squad screeched to a stop in the middle of the street.

Captain Caruso pulled up in his red pickup. He climbed out and slammed the door. The front windows of the house broke, glass blowing outward in a shower of glittery sparks. "Burning hot, boys. Get some water through those windows."

J.T. moved a little closer to the house, with Santos right behind him. More sirens wailed in the distance. Ladder 2—finally.

Captain Caruso gave Matt a speculative look. "Who wants to blow you up, son?"

Matt felt the words in his gut. "Sir, I'm not sure I know what you mean."

"Frank, get over here," Caruso yelled to the captain of the bomb squad. "Clark, who goes in first on every fire?"

"I don't ask the men to go anyplace I'm not willing to go first." Matt crossed his arms over his chest. Just exactly what was Caruso implying? He wasn't a glory hog. They all had their jobs and he and Lara went in first on the pipe.

The captain of the bomb squad jogged up, small scope in his hands. "No way to tell if they are explosives from here."

Caruso turned to him. "Johnson, help us out. Clark here is first through the door on every scene, or at least often enough for it to be a pattern."

Johnson rubbed a finger across his already-smooth mustache. "So if someone rigged that door to blow, it's possible that you or your partner were the target. You been digging around on this meth case?"

"Yes, sir, I'm working on the task force, but so are seven other people."

Captain Caruso poked Matt, his booming voice loud over the roar of the fire. "It makes as much sense as anything else. You need to think back at what buttons you been pushing, see if you can figure out which one triggered this."

Lara jogged up beside them, holding her helmet on with one hand, her cheeks bright pink from the heat.

"Sir, with all due respect, we don't even know if there are explosives—"

The house blew in an enormous fireball, sucking all the energy out of the air. For one split second of frozen inactivity they all stood in shock before a wave of heat and debris blasted over them. Matt hit the ground, tucking his head in to allow his helmet to protect his head and neck.

As the immediate impact passed, Matt looked to the side to see the captain and Johnson from the bomb squad flat on the asphalt with their arms over their heads.

To his left, Lara had flattened herself against the far side of the fire truck.

He rolled to his feet. He guessed that answered the question of whether or not there were explosives in the building. "You guys okay?"

Caruso's mouth was moving, but Matt couldn't hear him. He shook his head, holding a hand out for the captain's. He pulled Caruso to his feet and turned back to help Johnson up, but all Matt saw was the back of his bulletproof vest as he walked away, screaming into a walkie-talkie.

Lara reached his side. "This is getting old."

He grimaced, the ringing in his ears reduced to a slightly lower decibel. "No kidding. The captain thinks maybe we were the target."

"Seriously? Because of the drug case?" Ash floated and drifted in the air around Lara like fat black snowflakes.

Matt shrugged and sent a look back at the house, now a burning shell. It wouldn't last much longer despite the fact that Ladder 2 was now on scene to help them drown the sucker.

The hot burning fire after the explosion quickly exhausted most of the fuel, so within forty-five minutes the crew had the fire down to smoldering timbers standing in a lake of sooty water. Santos and J.T. would walk through what remained with some of the crew from Ladder 2, but there was little to no chance of a rekindle with what there was left.

Matt would begin collecting evidence as soon as Maria Fuentes arrived. He walked to the truck to retrieve his shovel. He would go through the remains of the house with the CSI.

"So the captain thinks we may be, what, the target of some drug conspiracy?" He turned to see Lara shrugging out of her Nomex coat, her ocean-colored eyes glowing on her soot-blackened face.

"I guess. And to tell you the truth, I started

out thinking the idea was crazy, but it doesn't seem so insane when you consider what just happened. And what probably would've happened when we knocked down that door."

"The target could be the owner of the house." Lara pulled a peppermint out of her uniform pants and opened the wrapper.

"Don't forget the house was foreclosed. It would probably be more likely that the house was burned *by* the owner."

She popped the candy in her mouth. "Yeah, but if that's the case, why rig it to blow?"

"That's the problem."

"And our evidence just burned to the ground."

"Yep." Matt shifted the shovel to his other hand. "Chances are we'll find something, but regardless, it gives us a starting place. Somewhere along the way these past couple of days, we've stepped on some toes. I think that means we've been doing our job right."

"Well, by all means, let's continue." She grinned, a slash of white in a dirty face making his heart do a long, lazy flip.

She started toward the destroyed house but then stopped and turned back to Matt. "Maybe we should talk to Baby J. I think he probably knows a lot more than he's telling. He doesn't strike me as the type to let a new drug enter his marketplace and not have his finger on it."

"He may not want to talk to me. Sure, he feels like he owes me, but in his business, if you tell the wrong person the wrong thing, it can get you killed."

Her hazel eyes were serious. "I refuse to let them scare me off, but at this rate it could be us that gets killed."

Matt stared after her as she walked back toward the house. There was just something about her, some courageous sense of honor, that drew him to her. Like a moth to a flame, he didn't seem to be able to stay away.

And now he'd be taking her out on a date, thanks to J.T. and Santos, who thought they were playing a joke. Some joke. It was a dream for him.

But he'd been singed by her once. He knew better than to believe that there was any feeling on her part but friendship. Assuming anything else would be wishful thinking. And with his job on the line, both here and at the police department, he didn't have the luxury of making mistakes.

At the end of her shift, Lara was packing her bag for home when her cell phone rang.

Her mother's voice, shrill and excited, came through. "Mom, slow down, I can't understand you."

"Someone was on the porch." Her mother took a deep breath. "I thought I heard footsteps on the porch, but when I looked, no one was there. Then a few minutes later, I heard a crash. Your planter fell off the porch rail. It's in pieces on the sidewalk."

Lara waved a silent goodbye to the crew sitting around the kitchen table and kept talking as she walked to her car. "You didn't go outside, did you, Mom?"

"No. I can see it out the window."

The summer beach traffic was horrendous, but she only lived a few blocks away from the fire house. She could be there in minutes. "Make sure the doors are all locked. I'll probably be home before you finish checking the windows and doors."

Lara's palm around the cell phone was sweaty. She didn't want to scare her mother, but this was just what she and Matt were talking about. This investigation, for reasons known only to "the bad guys," had put her and Matt at the center of their crosshairs.

"I checked the doors. They're locked." Her

mother's voice, though still breathless, had lost the edge of hysteria.

Lara shot into traffic on the main road. Horns blared. Welcome to the beach. She didn't have time for this. "Hang on, Mom. I'll be home quick as I can."

She risked her life turning left across traffic into her neighborhood. "I'm turning on our street now. Check the windows. I'll use my key to come in. You're going to be fine, right?"

"Right. I'm good. You can hang up now." Her mom sounded steady, in control.

"See you in a sec." Lara hung up the phone as she pulled in her driveway. Before getting out of the car, she eyed the area surrounding her little cottage. She couldn't see the front door from this position, but everything else looked clear.

Yet someone had definitely been sneaking around. As her mom had said, one of her planters was smashed into a thousand pieces on the sidewalk. She couldn't see the other one, so she could only guess that it was the one that her mother could see smashed on the front porch.

She laced her fingers through her keys and started for the door. Keys as a weapon would not be effective against, oh, say a gun, but in hand to hand, it could be the second's difference that would save her life.

On the steps of the porch she stalled out. Yeah, she would definitely say someone was trying to send her a message. In huge letters on the side of her house someone had written STOP OR DIE. Subtle.

They'd tried to kill her and missed, so here was a new message at her house. She whispered a prayer of thanks that they'd all made it through and that her mom hadn't been hurt even though she'd been home. She started to put her key in the lock and stopped. "And I'm sorry if I was a little cranky about the traffic."

She took one last look at the block letters on the pretty siding of her house. Honestly, it made her mad instead of afraid. It made her more determined to find these creeps and put them away.

Sliding the key fully into the lock, she opened the door. "Mom?"

Her mother, slim and pretty in khakis and a summer sweater, came into the living room, a cup clutched in her hands. *Oh, please, God, if you don't mind one more prayer, please don't let her be drinking.*

"I made some tea. My hands were shaking." Her mother smiled, but the effort was visible.

Lara crossed the room and hugged her mom. She couldn't remember the last time she had.

She'd spent so much time being embarrassed, mad, hurt, disappointed. All those negative emotions that were definitely justified, definitely real. But also real was the fear churning in her stomach that something could have happened to her mom, home alone. "I'm really glad you're all right. I was worried."

The surprise on her mom's face made Lara's throat burn.

Ava lifted the mug. "Do you want some?"

Lara swallowed hard. "No, thanks. Listen, Matt and I are working a case with the Sea Breeze Police Department. We're not sure who's behind all this, but we know there are some very dangerous people involved. It could be that coming to the house was just the first warning. Next time they may not be so polite."

The words on the house made that pretty clear.

"Why can't you arrest them?" Her mother's slender fingers had gone white around the mug.

"We will, when we have evidence." When we know who they are. "But if you want to go to a hotel, I can arrange it for you."

Her mom thought for a minute, the narrow bridge between her eyebrows wrinkling. "I haven't had a home in a long time. For the first time in ages I feel like I have one here. I don't want to leave, if you're okay with me being here."

The words again cut straight to the heart. She'd been the one to deprive her mother of a home, petitioning the court at just age eighteen to take over the family "assets" to feed herself and her nine-year-old sister when her mother was off on constant benders.

She'd known even then that it was her mother's effort to self-medicate, to erase the pain that she felt because of her illness. But she could never understand why she and Emmy weren't enough of a reason to stay sober.

Those days were behind them. Her mom was on the path to recovery and she was doing great. Lara smiled and, with her arm still around her mom, gave her a squeeze. "Sounds good. I don't want you to leave, not until you're ready. But I need to call Matt and then the police to report this."

"Will they do anything?"

"They'll make a record of it. The next call I'm making is to an alarm company. I think it's time we had an alarm installed." Because she was dead certain that she and Matt weren't going to stop their investigation, regardless of the threat on the side of the house. A threat the bad guys would like nothing more than to make good on.

SEVEN

The rest of his crew long gone, Matt sat on the tailgate of the captain's truck in the driveway of the burned shell of a house. He dialed Baby J's number again. It went straight to voice mail. Again.

His phone rang. Finally.

"Matt Clark."

"Matt, it's Lara."

Her voice sounded tight, very un-Lara.

"What's going on?" He didn't have a sister, but he had a mom and he knew that thick voice meant something was wrong, very wrong, and it made him want to kick someone into gear.

"Apparently the people who planted the wire at the house wanted to make sure we got the message. They spray painted it on my house."

White-hot anger speared through Matt, but he leveled it with effort. "What did it say?"

"Basically, back off or suffer the consequences."

"Exactly what, Lara?"

She hesitated. Then, "Stop or die."

He rolled to his feet to pace the driveway. "Get your things together."

"What? No." She gentled her voice. "Matt, listen, they didn't break in, just left the message. And I've already called an alarm company. They're coming tomorrow evening to set things up."

He didn't like it, but he knew her well enough to know that there would be no breaking through when she'd made up her mind. "Will you at least call Cruse Conyers and get him to send his patrol cars by throughout the night?"

"Already done."

"Good." He took a deep breath and forced himself to give her the room he knew she needed, just like he had every day, every hour for the last six months.

"Have you gotten in touch with Baby J?"

"No, not for lack of trying, though." After saying goodbye, he hung up the phone and looked back over his notes.

He'd recorded the interviews he'd taken with the other firefighters at the scene and with the bystanders who had come outside to watch. In the middle of the day not many neighbors had been home and the ones that had—well, they weren't the type to give a cop details. Picking up his pencil, he scribbled a note about the cars on the street when they arrived on scene.

Maria Fuentes and a couple of her crime-scene investigators had come and gone. He and Maria had sifted through the piles of soot and ash in the house, looking for evidence. They'd found several triggering devices, the remains of batteries and lots and lots of shrapnel—the remains of a pipe bomb or several.

He liked doing this kind of work. It was interesting working with Maria and he liked the investigational aspect of the job. What he didn't like was that if he took the job on a per-manent basis, he would no longer be working as a firefighter.

Being a firefighter was pretty much all he'd ever wanted. All those years when his brothers were picking on him for being the weakling, he'd dreamed of rescuing people. When they were playing cops and robbers, he was pretend-ing to put out fires.

As the arson investigator, he would have other people on his team. Crime-scene investigators like Maria and police officers like Joe Sheehan. He'd work more closely with the senior officers in the fire department. It would be challenging, new, different. In many ways more like police work than fighting fires. But as he came face-to-face with the possibility of losing his crew today, he wasn't sure he was ready to give up his career as a firefighter and working with them. His gut was twisted up in knots.

The phone at his waist rang. Lara again? He checked the readout, but the number was blocked. "Matt Clark."

"Matt, it's J. Did you find what you were looking for?"

"What do you mean?" For some reason, Matt clicked on the small recorder that he used to conduct interviews.

"Did you find your friend's sister?" Not that Matt knew him all that well, but Baby J's voice sounded strange, quiet.

"No. We checked all the places we knew to check plus the ones you told us about. Found nothing. At least nothing that would lead us to Emmy." *I'm no narc.* The words came back to Matt from his conversation with Baby J the other day. Regardless, as soon as they found Emmy, Matt would be reporting the worst of the houses that they went into, if for nothing else than to hope that mother and baby got the help they needed.

J went silent, so quiet that Matt almost thought he'd hung up, but then he spoke even more softly into the phone. "There's one more place you can check, but you'd have to go now. Later might be too late."

"Why?" Matt cradled the phone to his neck and flipped a page in his notebook.

"Let's just say there are people who wouldn't want you to get her out. And that card I gave you isn't going to do you any good. Not there." His voice shook.

"Give me an address."

J whispered an address into the phone, then added, "Don't call me again, Matt. I know I owe you, but talking to you will get us both killed."

The phone clicked in Matt's ear with finality. He'd already put his tools in the truck the captain left for him, so he ripped the page with the address from the notebook and dug the keys out of his pocket.

If J was telling the truth, Matt had only a small window of time to get to Emmy. He was going into a dangerous situation with no backup and had no idea what to expect.

The ranch-style house was only a few blocks away from the latest fire. As he pulled up, he realized there was a distinct difference in this house and the one that had been so bad the other day. It wasn't in the nicest of neighborhoods, but the grass was cut, the lawn was edged and, although there were a few cars, there were no people hanging around outside.

Matt drove past the house and parked down the block, taking the time to walk the perimeter before going to the door. Maybe a badge would get him in the door—if he had one. More likely it would just get him shot.

No movement. The place looked deserted. Matt walked up the steps to the front door, took a deep breath and walked in. The living area was decorated with one big leather couch and some folding chairs and a huge flat-screen television hung on one wall. Half-empty chip bags and soda cans, along with the occasional beer can, littered the room.

His steps silent on the carpeted floor, he rounded the corner into the kitchen. Drug paraphernalia lay on the table. A mirror, a razor blade, some orange powder. The new drug. The kids had been right. Bright Orange did look like a drink mix.

And it looked like he was in the right place. He opened a cabinet and found a small stack of little zipper-closed bag and a scale.

He glanced at his watch. Three minutes had

passed already since he arrived at the house. He stopped and listened.

Down the hall were several closed doors. Every instinct he had said, *Get out of here now.* And it had crossed his mind, after the booby trap set for his team today, that J could be setting him up.

Matt set his jaw and flung open the first door. Empty. The second, also empty. He closed his eyes and took in a deep breath. Okay, one more door at the end of the hall.

He didn't have a weapon, didn't really want one, but the hair on his arms prickled. He'd been in enough dangerous situations that he'd learned to trust his intuition—which was at this moment telling him he was crazy to be in this house.

At the door, Matt turned the knob, not making a sound. He swung it open carefully. And let the breath he didn't know he'd been holding out. A blonde sprawled on the bed, jeans and tank top dirty, the items she'd used to shoot up on the bed beside her, a tourniquet still wrapped around her arm. It wasn't the first time he'd seen them—he'd been called out plenty of times for overdoses—but every time, it made him scream inside.

Matt gently eased the girl to her back. She

looked exactly like Lara, but hard living had taken a toll on her. Her hair was dull and lifeless, her eyes stained with dark circles and her lips cracked and bleeding. If he hadn't known to look for it, he never would've seen the resemblance.

He shook her shoulder. "Emmy. Wake up. Come on, it's time to go."

She didn't move. Her breaths were shallow. He put two fingers to her neck, searching for a pulse. Her skin was diaphoretic, her pulse thready. And way too fast.

"Emmy, wake up." She still didn't move. He glanced at his watch. Nine minutes. He needed to get out of here.

Emmy needed medical care. He and Lara could give it to her, but first he needed to get her in the car. He lifted her into his arms just as he heard the front door open and male voices, several of them, talking.

Adrenaline dumped into his system in one vicious push, sending his own pulse skyrocketing.

Matt laid Emmy back on the bed, her arms flopping to the side. Creeping to the door, he pushed the lock. He just bought himself a couple of seconds. Maybe.

The windows, low to the ground in this

one-story house, would have to do for an exit. Assuming no one saw him, he could step out and then reach back in for Emmy.

So many things had to go right.

He clicked open the window lock and pushed up with the other hand. Waiting around would only get him deeper in trouble. If the guys in the other room found him here, he was dead. He didn't know what she was doing here or how she got mixed up with them, but her color was getting worse and her breathing almost nonexistent.

The guys in the front were getting louder.

He had to move now.

He lifted her in his arms again. She was dead weight, her head lolling back. He placed her closer to the window and stepped outside. When he could get an arm underneath her, he pulled her out the window.

Okay, not ideal. His back strained at the awkward weight. But getting her out where he could treat her had to be the first priority. When he had her on the ground outside, he slid the window closed. Quickly he moved her into the classic fireman's carry over his shoulders.

Matt booked it toward the department truck. He struggled to hear over the pulse thundering in his ears. Did a shout come from behind him?

At the truck, he shifted Emmy so he could hold her wrist with his right hand and dig the keys out of his pocket with his left.

He glanced back at the house. The front door was still closed and the house quiet, but there the luck ended. A car, a black Ford Mustang, had pulled up in front of the house.

A tall, lanky guy got out of the car. He slammed the door and looked straight at Matt.

Matt froze, waiting for the man to sound the alarm. A black baseball cap was pulled low over the dude's face, making it impossible to see his features.

But Matt stared. Something about him looked familiar. The walk, the body shape, something.

Shaking it off, he opened the door and flopped Emmy onto the passenger seat. She started the slow slide down, but he strapped her in. She was in bad shape.

Matt jumped in his side of the truck and started it up, praying nonstop. Scattered, disjointed prayers, but God knew what he meant, knew what Emmy needed even more than he did. And although Matt didn't even know Emmy, God did. And loved her, despite all the abuse she'd suffered.

At the next stoplight, he reached over to take

Emmy's pulse again. As he did, her body stiffened and she began to seize.

Just like the girl they'd lost.

Heart racing triple-time, Lara ran for the emergency room door. She'd jumped in the car as soon as she got Matt's message that he was at the hospital with Emmy. The doors slid open and she barreled through them.

Hard arms caught her up. She pushed away.

"Lara. Stop, honey. It's okay, she's gonna be okay." He held her shoulders and looked into her eyes. The concern she saw there put her over the edge.

"I thought—" Her voice caught on a sob. She fisted her hand, pressed it to her mouth.

Matt didn't say anything, just wrapped his arms around her and pulled her in to his chest. She thought, just for a second, that she shouldn't be in his arms, that she should be strong. But beneath her ear she could hear his heartbeat, steady and sure. And it made her feel safe.

"I found her about an hour ago at the place J told me to look. I would've called you, but he said there was only a window of a few minutes. As it was she was in bad shape, but I thought maybe between the two of us…"

"What happened?" More steady now thanks

to Matt's reassuring presence, she was able to get past the first frantic "I've got to get to the hospital" moments.

"She had a seizure in the car. I brought her straight here. They had a tough time getting her stabilized, but if she makes it through the night, she should be okay."

Lara drew in a deep breath, probably the first one since she'd heard that Emmy was missing. "Where is she?"

"She's in Trauma 2, but they're going to move her to ICU in a few minutes."

"Can you call her husband? He should know we're here." She dug around in her pocket for the slip of paper Ben had given her. He should know, but oh, what a hard road he had ahead of him.

"Absolutely. What about your mom?"

"Tomorrow will be soon enough. She's had a tough day. I left her at home with a cop sitting in front of the house." Lara stopped midway to the trauma room then came back. She tried to focus on his face, but she couldn't see through the haze of tears.

"Oh, babe." He reached for her again, rubbing her arms.

"I didn't say thank you." She chewed her lip, trying and failing to hold in the emotion. One skinny tear tracked down her face. *"Thank you."*

"It was nothing, Bump." He shrugged off her praise.

She laughed and swiped the evidence off her face. "I have a feeling it was a little more than nothing."

He just shook his head. "Go see your sister. Once they move her, you won't be able to stay with her. I'll go call, what's his name?"

"Ben."

"Right. I'll be back, Lara. I won't leave you here alone."

Lara watched him walk away, his broad shoulders willing to take on whatever she would let him. He didn't deserve this, didn't deserve the crap that being her friend brought along with it. And that was what she'd been afraid of all along, that he would get splattered with the drama that was inevitably her life.

She blew out a breath and turned toward the door of the trauma room, stalling as she got closer. She laid her palms on the glass. Her baby sister lay in the bed, tubes going everywhere, her arms held tight by restraints. She must've fought them. She'd always been a tough cookie. She'd had to be.

"I talked to the doctor. She's going to be

okay." Lara turned to see Matt's mom, the hospital administrator. "There will be a long road of recovery, but she'll survive this. You both will. We're going to make sure she gets the help she needs."

The sweet voice had steel underneath. In her trim summer suit and high-heeled shoes, Mrs. Clark looked capable and smart. Nothing at all like Lara felt. Lara wanted to sink into the floor. The very thing that she'd tried to avoid—having her life exposed to the people she respected— had happened. It was her worst nightmare.

Her face felt like it might crack, but she forced a smile. "I know she will. It's hard to see her like this."

"Life is hard. Unbearably so sometimes." Mrs. Clark laid a soft hand on Lara's back. "But I've found in situations like this that holding on to God and trusting Him gives me strength."

She couldn't quite manage the smile this time. Maybe that was true for some people, but for her reality was a better bet.

Mrs. Clark took one last look through the window at Emmy. "I have got to get back to work, but I've been trying to get Matt to bring you to dinner at my house. How does tomorrow night sound?"

Lara opened her mouth, definitely intending

to say no. Facing Matt's perfect family over dinner wasn't her idea of a great evening, especially with everything that had happened.

"Now don't say no. You'll hurt my feelings. I'll see you both around six. Oh, and don't bring anything. I never cook for company. Just don't tell Matt's dad. He thinks I have moments of brilliance. So you'll be there?"

She was beginning to understand where Matt got his leadership skills. "Sure?"

"Great. And, Lara, I'm praying for you. I always pray for you and Matt and for your safety, but I'm saying a special prayer for you and your sister tonight." Mrs. Clark gave her a quick hug and walked away.

Without giving herself time to back out, Lara opened the door to the trauma room. The white walls were sterile and empty, giving the illusion that nothing moved in this room, but there was so much going on here. Her sister lay fighting for life. But which life would she come back to? The life with a husband and baby, the life where she was a happy mom and college student? Or to the life of a drug addict? It was hard to know.

The respirator whooshed and the machines beeped, keeping track of Emmy's blood pressure and pulse. There was no machine to measure the pain of watching Emmy's wrong choices eat her up. It was worse than if Lara had experienced them herself. She longed to make things better for Emmy, even as she wanted to shake her. It didn't make any sense.

At her involuntary sigh, the nurse looked up from where she'd been adjusting the tape on the IV catheter. "I'll give you a couple minutes."

Lara couldn't take her eyes off Emmy. Her sister was intubated and lines ran all different directions, but Lara was used to seeing that. Knowing what all those tubes did and not being terrified when they were attached to someone she loved was a whole different thing.

Emmy looked so fragile—dark blue stains under her eyes, cracked lips, skin broken and blistered.

It was so needless. Lara clenched her fist. *Why? Why, God, am I able to go into a burning building and save a complete stranger, but I can't save my own sister?*

A sob choked out. *Please, God, help her get well. She deserves to be happy.*

The door opened behind her. When Matt stepped into the room, she didn't stop to think, just reached out to grip his hand. It'd been such a long week and she was so exhausted. And that surely was the only reason it seemed so easy to hold on to him like a lifeline.

Because she didn't have *those* kinds of feelings for Matt. But oh, did it feel nice to have someone to hold her hand, someone to be strong for her, when for her entire life she'd been the strong one, the one holding things together. Or trying.

He squeezed her fingers. "They're ready to take her upstairs. You okay?"

"Yeah. It's hard seeing her like this. She was such an adorable kid. She wanted to be a ballerina." Lara picked up Emmy's hand with her free one and ran her thumb over the ragged fingernails. "When I was thirteen, I scraped together enough change to buy some old ballet slippers at the thrift store. She wore one of my mother's old nightgowns for a tutu. You would've thought she was a princess the way she danced around the house."

"You were a great big sister."

"I wasn't. I didn't protect her."

Matt turned her to face him. "Honey, could you even protect yourself?"

"It doesn't matter. I should've protected Emmy. Maybe it would've been different for her—if I had." Her voice caught. "I really wish things had been different for her."

The door opened and the nurses and orderlies came into the room. "I'm sorry, we're going to have to ask you to leave. She'll be upstairs in ICU, but visiting hours aren't until in the morning."

Lara leaned forward to kiss Emmy's head, the way she'd done when Emmy was a tiny girl. A tear dropped onto her cheek. "I love you. Be strong, baby girl."

"Come on, I'll follow you home." Matt held the door open for Lara. In the hall, she collapsed into one of the bright orange vinyl chairs. A faded fake palm tree sagged in the corner. It looked like she felt.

"I'll be fine." She wiped her face on her sleeve.

"I know you will." He followed her out of the E.R.

"But you're going to follow me home anyway?" She pulled her keys out of her jeans pocket.

Matt pretended to tip his nonexistent hat. "Why, yes, ma'am, I am."

She would be okay. She had to believe it because if she didn't keep telling herself that, she was afraid she might fall apart at the seams.

EIGHT

A uniformed police officer showed Matt the interview room. After a late-night phone call last night, he and Cruse Conyers had agreed that they needed to bring Baby J in for questioning. J had given him Emmy's location, but he was the best, right now *only,* lead they had to bring them closer to finding who was behind the Bright Orange hitting the streets.

Department psychologist Gracie VanDoren was already in the room. Matt had met her—briefly—before, so he shook her hand before resting his hands on the windowsill of the two-way mirror and leaning in. "Did I miss anything?"

She shook her head, short, blond, Meg Ryan curls bouncing around her face. "Not a thing. So far Mr. McElroy is refusing to talk."

"Mr. McElroy?"

She pointed through the window. "Our subject? James McElroy."

"Baby J."

A tiny dimple appeared in the corner of her bottom lip. "If you must."

Cruse was seated across the table from J, whom Matt could see through the two-way mirror. J was dressed in his typical khakis, this time with a white button-down, the sleeves rolled up, a leather banded watch with a gold face showing at his left wrist.

"This is a friendly question-and-answer session," Cruse began. In contrast, Conyers was dressed in jeans and a ratty T-shirt, with black leather boots on his feet rather than the Docksiders that his detainee wore.

"I'm not answering any questions." J stared at a spot on the wall.

"Let's just start with an easy one." Cruse pulled a photo of the house where they'd found Emmy from the pile. "You know this place?"

J looked at the picture and shrugged.

"What about this man?" The police captain slid the picture of the suspect from the original fire across the table.

Baby J, mouth tightly closed, simply looked at Cruse, no expression on his face.

"He's afraid of something." Gracie stepped

closer to the mirror. "I'd have to check the video, but when Cruse asked that last question, his eyes widened and dilated."

Cruse stared at J and scratched his chin. "How did you know where Emmy Payne was?"

James McElroy blinked, leaning back in his chair and crossing his arms.

Cruse closed the file folder, walked to the door and pressed the button for the intercom. "Okay, set up the bodyguard in the room next door. We're done here."

Matt heard J's indrawn breath. "Stop."

Cruse turned around. "Yeah?"

"I know you don't like me or respect me, but one thing you have to understand is that I protect my people." His bright blue eyes were no longer jumpy. He looked directly at Cruse. "I went to the house and I saw her there."

Cruse tapped his pencil on the table. "What led you to go to that particular house?"

"You know how it is, dude. I'm a business-man. I hear things, I check it out. I heard these guys were selling out of that house and went to check it out. I thought they might be some serious competition. I was wrong."

"You weren't wrong about them selling the Bright Orange, though."

J flipped his bangs out of his eyes with a

jerk of the head. He laughed. "Bright Orange. Stupid name for a drug. Yeah, they had some. But they're not the guys you're looking for."

He glanced at the mirror. Matt could've sworn he looked right at him.

"Names," Cruse ordered.

"I don't think he's telling the truth." Gracie stepped closer to the glass, her gold necklace swinging toward the window.

"Ya think?" Matt shoved his hands in his pockets. "Sorry, I'm sorry. It's just—J is probably the only person in town who actually knows anything about this drug besides the people who are actually doing this and he isn't talking. Meanwhile, people are dying."

Gracie turned her back to the glass and faced Matt, a sunny smile on her face. "I understand. It's tough to be a rescuer and know that, in this case, you're already behind the curve when you get called out."

Just like that, she'd nailed it. Spooky. "Um, yeah."

The door opened and shut behind Conyers. "We need to get this guy out of here. Maybe we'll get more from having him followed than asking him questions. Gracie, I'd appreciate your impressions once you have time to review the tapes. Matt, you have a minute?"

"Sure." Matt followed Cruse to his office, waving a goodbye to Gracie. "What's up?"

"The property is bank-owned, so that's consistent with the other two places we've connected with them. It's not very hard to get a list of foreclosed properties, so that doesn't help us much, but we'll keep checking the homes on the list we have." Cruse's desk chair squeaked as he settled in it.

"What does the DEA have to say about all this? Are we still planning to bring someone in on the case?"

Cruse studied the picture of his wife on his desk. Without looking at Matt, he said, "They have someone on the ground. That's all they would tell me. I understand need-to-know and I figure if we get in their way, they'll let us know."

"That's probably an understatement." He leaned on the door frame and crossed his arms.

"We've had teams watching the house where you found Emmy, but so far no one has gone back there. I guess they got spooked by the fact that we knew she was there." He rubbed the heels of his hands over his eyes. "My worst fear is that they'll decide the water's getting too hot here and move on somewhere else."

"Any leads on the guns we found in the house?"

"We handed those over to the army's investigative team. If they can trace them back to the source, maybe that'll give us a starting point." Cruse pushed away from his desk and stood. "We'll kick Baby J and the bodyguard loose for now."

"Cruse, is it possible that Baby J was trying to start a new venture with Bright Orange?" It wasn't something Matt wanted to believe, but he had to at least throw the idea out there. So far, J was the only person with information.

The weight of the job showed in the craggy lines of the lieutenant's face. "Possible, but not probable. We've been watching James McElroy a long time. I don't think he has the connections for this type of job. Maybe I'm wrong."

He looked at the picture of his wife again. "My wife is pregnant, did you know that?"

Matt grinned. "No. Congratulations. Life is about to change in the Conyers household."

"That it will." Cruse's smile disappeared as fast as it had appeared on his face. "But I won't let these people pollute the town where I'll be bringing my baby girl home. That's for sure."

As Matt left the building, he considered the conversation with Cruse. There was a lot at stake. Emmy's life hung in the balance. And many more were at risk if they didn't catch these criminals and get this drug off the streets.

Driving the street that ran along the beach after her twenty-four-hour shift used to be a time to unwind, a time Lara treasured. Even a glimpse of the sparkling surf and emerald-green ocean had always been like taking a deep breath.

Lately, though, she didn't seem to be able to get her mind off everything going on. Today, instead of out there in the foamy surf, her heart had been at the hospital with her baby sister.

The news was good. Emmy was doing a little better, her blood pressure more stable. If she continued to improve, they'd move her out of ICU in the morning.

Matt hadn't been at work today, instead sending Brian from B shift to fill in for him. But he'd texted her that he was working on some leads. He wanted to talk to Emmy together later. And he would pick her up at six for dinner.

What she needed was a bubble bath and an uneventful night in front of mindless television. She definitely didn't need a night with Matt's picture-perfect family, no matter how nice Mrs. Clark was.

Lara pulled into her driveway, rolling slowly to a stop. Something wasn't right.

Glass lay in glittery shards on her front porch. She ran for the house, leaving her car door standing open. "Mom?"

She knew she shouldn't go in the house, but her mom had been home. Quickly, she pressed 911 and told the dispatcher her address. "Someone broke into my house. The front window is broken and the door is cracked."

The dispatcher called for police units in the background. "You weren't home when the break-in happened?"

"No, but I think my mom might've been home. I need to go in the house to check."

The dispatcher's voice remained calm and brisk. "Ma'am, I'd advise that you stay on the porch until the officers arrive."

Yeah, she'd advise that, too. Her stomach revolted. She dropped the phone and ran for the bushes.

After a few minutes, she picked the phone up. "I have to check. I'll stay on the line."

The front door was cracked open. The glass had come from the window, but everything in her house had been trashed. Every picture was in pieces, every cushion tumbled onto the floor. "Mom?"

A footstep crunched on the glass outside. She ducked into the hall. She wanted so badly to tell the dispatcher that someone was at the door, but she couldn't risk it. Instead, she pushed the end button on the phone and cut off communication with the only person who knew she was here. Her heart slammed against her ribs, clammy sweat breaking out on her forehead. She flattened herself against the wall, trying to keep her breathing quiet.

From her hiding place in the hall, she heard the intruder enter her living room. Slow footsteps ground on the broken picture frames.

"Lara?" Matt's voice was steady, but because she knew him she could hear the undercurrent of stress. "Lara, where are you?"

She let out the breath she'd been holding and stepped out. "I'm here."

"I heard the call on the scanner. You scared me." He walked closer, his every muscle standing out against his soft T-shirt, his alert stance telegraphing his unhappiness. "What happened?"

"Matt, I don't know where my mom is." Her voice was high and tight, the edge of panic beginning to rise in her throat again.

His eyebrows twitched together but he just

said, "There's probably a perfectly reasonable explanation. Did you check all the rooms?"

"No. I didn't have time."

"Okay, I'll do that while you look around and see if maybe there's a clue here to where your mom went. We'll have to be careful not to disturb evidence or Maria will skin us, but maybe there's something that will help."

She nodded, her lip caught between her teeth, not trusting herself to talk anymore. Her throat ached with unshed tears, the fear for her mother so real and present.

Matt picked his way into the bedrooms. She could hear him calling her mother's name. *Oh, Mom, where are you? Please be okay.*

Lara looked around the living room, forcing herself to concentrate on what might tell her where her mom was. The mess would have to wait.

"She's not in the back." Matt's voice was serious. "But that's probably good, right? It means she wasn't here when they came."

"Why didn't the alarm go off?" She picked up a broken picture frame and dropped it back on the pile. "Unless she *was* here and didn't have it on."

Matt held her arms, his voice firm and calm. "Don't borrow trouble. There's no sign that she's been injured. Let's keep looking. Okay? I'll start in the kitchen."

"How would we know if there had been a struggle?" She couldn't let it go. She was so, so scared.

"Hey, look, Bump, I found a note on the floor. It must've been by the phone." Matt walked into the room carrying a sheet from a sticky pad. "She says she's going to the hospital to sit in the ICU waiting room for visiting hours."

Relief poured over her like a balm. What could've happened hadn't. *Thank you, God.* "I'm calling to see if she's really there, but I'm so glad she wasn't here."

The flash of lights outside caught her eye. She walked to the steps. The cop coming up her walk was unmistakable with his shaved head and silver-lensed sunglasses. "Hi, Joe."

"Lara. Dispatch said you had a break-in? Guess I don't really have to ask, do I? This place is a mess."

"Yeah, the whole house was pretty much trashed."

"Anything missing?" He pulled a small notebook from his back pocket.

"My mom wasn't here when I got home, so I didn't really think past that. We found out she's at the hospital, so I can check around now."

She looked at Matt leaning against the kitchen counter and then back to the cop.

Joe Sheehan smiled and tucked his sunglasses into the pocket of his uniform shirt, revealing smoky-gray eyes.

While Joe did a quick search of the remaining rooms of the house, Lara confirmed her mom was at the hospital. She looked around. It seemed like everything was there, but who could tell with the house looking like the "before" pictures in *The Messiest House in America?*

She didn't do helpless well, not since she was a kid. Those out-of-control days were behind her. In the absence of the bad guys, she wanted to punch something—anything.

"Hey, Lara?" Matt's voice came from behind the sofa.

"What are you doing back there?"

Matt's hand appeared first, followed by his head. "Is there a computer that goes to this power cord?"

Her stomach sank. "My laptop. I haven't seen it."

Joe walked back into the living room, the small notepad back in his hands. "Where'd you leave it?"

"I always shut it down and leave it on the

coffee table when I go to work. Oh, no. Matt, I had notes from the investigation."

Joe jotted something down in the pad. "Do you think that's what your intruder was after?"

"I have no idea. Why would he focus on me, when there are seven other people on the task force, including the two of you?"

Matt's normally cheerful face chiseled into hard lines. "Maybe because he knows you saw him."

He and Joe shared a look and Lara knew what that meant. They were about to start making plans for her.

"You go pack your overnight bag and I'll call my mother and tell her you're staying over."

"No, Matt. I'm not going to impose on your mom like that."

"Believe me, it's no imposition. She'd be furious if I didn't offer." He looked at his watch. "We're supposed to be there for dinner right now anyway. You can fight it out with her over lasagna."

Joe shoved the little pad in his back pocket. "Now that's settled, I'm going outside to wait on Maria Fuentes and her Crime Scene Unit."

Lara raised her eyes to the ceiling. "I'll get

a bag, but I'm not staying at your mom's. And I'm taking my own car."

"Okay, okay. Hurry up. I'm hungry."

A chuckle at his impatience died as she took in the destruction in her bedroom. Not only had someone taken it apart, they had absolutely destroyed it. With such malice for her possessions, they'd surely just as easily harm her or her family if they got in the way.

NINE

Matt pushed open the door to his mom and dad's sprawling stucco house. "Hey, we're home."

No answer.

"My mom must not be home from picking up the takeout." He grinned.

Lara shot him a look from under her lashes. "She told me it was a secret."

"She thinks it is. And we love her, so we let her believe it. Come on, I'll show you around." He pushed open French doors into the recessed living area. "You can pretty much see the whole house from here except the bedrooms. When I was about ten, my mom wanted to move to a new house and my dad made her get this one remodeled instead because he didn't want to move. We ended up having to stay in a condo for three months, so my dad had to move out anyway."

He glanced back to catch Lara in a sigh. "What?"

"You have a great history. Family stories that are nice. I love all your mom's pictures." She walked into the living room, running her finger down the shiny brass banister rail.

"My brothers and I would get in trouble if we left fingerprints on that thing."

"Oh." Lara snatched her hand back and tucked it under her elbow, a horrified look on her face.

"Don't worry—she'll never know. We always had sticky fingers in those days. And, for what it's worth, all the stories aren't nice." He placed a hand on the small of her back and guided her toward the windows, nearly tripping over a backpack left in the middle of the floor.

Matt frowned down at it. "He's gonna catch it if that's still there when Mom gets home."

"Who?" There was a tiny frown between Lara's eyes.

"Marcus. My little brother." He walked to the window and looked into the backyard. "Where is that little fiend?"

The garage door slammed open and his mom struggled through it carrying four bags from Angelo's Italian Restaurant.

"Mom, let me help with that."

"There are two pans of lasagna in the car and don't think I didn't hear what you called Marcus."

Matt fought a smile and lost. His mom with her eagle ears. "Sorry. I won't do it again."

"I'm sure you won't. Now go get the lasagna."

"Yes, ma'am." Matt grabbed him mom's face between his hands and gave her a big smooch on both cheeks, leaving her laughing.

Lara crossed the room to Mrs. Clark as she started to unload the food, still laughing.

"That one will always be incorrigible. And charming, God love him." Setting the loaf of French bread on the counter, she put a soft hand on Lara's back. "I'm so glad that you could make it tonight. It's just family—with the exception of one of Reid's oldest friends."

Lara reached for the second bag of food, needing to do something to get rid of the awkwardness she felt. "Let me help you with those."

This time, Mrs. Clark threw her arms around Lara and squeezed. "What a delight you are. You watch. As soon as Matt brings the food in, he'll disappear."

Lara's cheeks heated. The easy affection between Mrs. Clark and Matt seemed to extend to her. It wasn't that she didn't like it—she did. She just felt so weird.

"I thought Matt was your youngest, Mrs. Clark." She'd never heard Matt talk about a little brother, but then she usually ran from discussions that included family.

"Please, it's Bethanne. We don't do anything formal around here, as I'm sure Matt has told you." She pulled another package of rolls out of the bag. "What were we talking about? Oh, yes. Marcus. He's a wonder."

Lara smiled at Bethanne Clark. She was so... positive. "How so?"

Matt pushed through the door with a lasagna on each arm. "Mom found Marcus at the hospital and brought him home."

Bethanne took one of the lasagnas and slid it into the oven, shaking her head. "Matthew, he's not a puppy we adopted. Marcus has juvenile diabetes. When he was ten years old, he was admitted to the hospital. The most adorable thing I'd ever seen." She stopped to put her hand on her hip, a dish towel hanging from her hand, forgotten. "Big soulful brown eyes, long curly eyelashes and a beautiful smile that he used to flirt with the nurses."

Matt pushed the other lasagna into the oven. "When Mom realized that no family had been to see Marcus and there was no one who would come in to learn about caring for him with diabetes, she started looking into his family situation. He'd been in the foster system for six years and was on his third home."

Bethanne took her jacket off and slung it around one of the kitchen chairs. She began to roll up her sleeves. "I intervened."

Matt grinned, his dark espresso eyes sparkling. "That's the nice way of putting it, but it's the best thing that ever happened to Marcus. And to our family. He's a great kid."

The door from the backyard slammed open and a teenage boy stormed through it, reaching with one hand to hike up his blue jeans. "Dude! I didn't know you were coming over. I got the new 'World in Flames' game yesterday. Wanna play?"

"I'd like to, bud, but I better help Mom with dinner." Matt tilted his head and shot a longing look at his mom, one that had probably been working on her since, oh, birth. Lara didn't even know if she'd be able to resist it and she was pretty tough.

"Mom, please?" Marcus wrapped long arms around his mother, his light brown skin glowing as he turned his face up to hers.

"I'll help you, Mrs. Clark," Lara said.

"Bethanne." Matt and his mom said it simultaneously, still staring at each other.

His mother gave in first, sighing and swatting Marcus on the shoulder. "Go. Play your game, but only if you've done your homework."

"Did it on the bus. Come on, Matt."

"Did you check your blood sugar?" his mother called after him.

He was already in the hall. "Yes, ma'am."

Matt flashed a grin and followed him across the living room. "Holler if you need me." He disappeared down the hall.

"As if." Mrs. Clark—Bethanne—stooped to get a salad bowl out from under the counter. "Matt has always managed to get out of his chores."

"Somehow that doesn't surprise me." He always tried to get out of them at the firehouse, too, but the guys always ganged up on him.

"But he's always been a joy." Bethanne thumped the wooden bowl on the counter, her no-nonsense moves quick and efficient. "Even when he was getting in trouble, he always had a smile on his face. Funny as it is, he and Marcus are probably the most alike of the four."

Lara glanced at the pictures on the wall. Four boys, three of them grown. "You have a great family."

Bethanne's face softened. "You don't think you do?"

"It's not like yours." Boy, was that the understatement of the year.

"Thank goodness for that. I'm not sure the world could handle more Clark men." She handed the roll of aluminum foil to Lara for the bread and began to slice a tomato for the salad.

Lara slid the roll of French bread out of the wrapper onto a piece of foil and began to butter it.

"You know my son loves you."

Lara whipped her head up to look at Bethanne Clark, her heart skipping a beat.

"I meant as a friend, darling girl. You deserve a friend." She walked to the oven, took a peek at the lasagna and adjusted the temperature. "The other, well now, that's between the two of you."

It was sweet, what Matt's mom was trying to do. And maybe all that had happened this week was too much. The tears welled. Because what Bethanne wished for would never happen.

It wasn't meant to be.

"My family isn't like yours," she started again, clenching her hand into a fist and then slowly, finger by finger, letting it go as she looked at the Clark family photo again.

Bethanne glanced at that picture, a shadow appearing in her eyes. "My goodness, that's a snapshot. We had to force Tyler into a tie. And Reid had to pay Ethan ten dollars to smile. You see what you want to see, Lara. My family is far from perfect. No family is. We all struggle to make it work."

Lara turned to place the bread in the oven beside the lasagna, hiding her face for just a moment. She had to tell Bethanne the truth. She couldn't let Matt's mom go on hoping for something that wouldn't—couldn't—happen. "My mom's bipolar."

"Oh, sweetheart." Bethanne poured two glasses of tea and clunked them on the table, easing into the seat closest to her with a sigh. She kicked off her heels and stretched her toes. "That feels good. Sit down. Was your mother diagnosed when you were a child?"

Lara nodded as she edged into a seat at Matt's family table, where he'd eaten a thousand meals growing up. If she looked closely, she could imagine babies teething on the edge of the table. She looked into Bethanne's friendly eyes, the image of Matt's. She could do this. For Matt.

"Was she on medication?"

"Not then. Mostly she tried to find ways to cope."

"Meaning she self-medicated. Alcohol?" Bethanne's perceptive eyes, chocolate velvet, looked into hers.

Admitting it was a relief. "Yes. And other things. But she's been on the meds for almost a year now and they've finally found a cocktail of meds that seems to work for her. She's doing a lot better. But with clarity of mind comes a kind of understanding of all the things you did that you can't take back. It's been a hard year for her."

"For you, too, if you're her primary caregiver."

Without warning, Lara's eyes overflowed. No one had known about her mother—she hadn't wanted the curious stares, the whispers, even the sympathy. But faced with Matt's mom's gentle care, she was tempted, so tempted, to let go of the tight rein she'd been keeping on herself and just feel.

She couldn't, of course. She still had Emmy to think about.

"You must've endured a lot being the oldest and having a sibling to look after. It explains so much about Emmy's addiction, too."

The kitchen door swung open. Matt backed

through it with an empty tea glass, shouting into the living room, "Okay, okay, I'll ask." He turned toward the table. "Hey, Mom. When's dinner ready? A certain someone who shall remain nameless says he's about to faint from hunger."

Lara quickly blinked back the tears as Bethanne bustled to the counter.

"Right now, Mr. Impatient. Tell Marcus to wash up and call your father and make sure he and Owen are on their way."

He grinned. "Done and done."

Matt didn't speak to Lara as he left the room, but he trailed a warm hand across her shoulders. She closed her eyes. She didn't deserve him, not even as a friend.

Bethanne pulled the lasagna out of the oven and eased it onto the counter. She turned to face Lara, tucking the pot holders under her arm. "You know, I haven't seen my son Tyler in three years."

Lara blinked, not knowing what to say. Her heart went out to Bethanne, who obviously loved her sons more than anything. "Did something happen?"

"Oh, I suppose it was the typical father-son thing. His dad wanted him to come on with the sheriff's department here. Tyler had other plans."

"You've had no word at all?"

"A phone call at Christmas. And on my birthday this year, I got a card." Bethanne opened the oven door and took out the other lasagna. "I console myself with the thought that no police officer has come knocking on my door. As long as that's the case, I'm pretty sure he's out there somewhere."

"That's so sad. I went a long time, almost a year without seeing Emmy. You just worry about them so much." Lara walked to the counter and picked up the salad bowl. "What about your middle son—Ethan, right?"

Bethanne's eyes instantly filled with tears. "Oh. I thought I was beyond that." She dabbed at her eyes with a dish towel. "Ethan's wife, Shawna, and their baby boy were killed two years ago. He, well, we've given him time, we've pestered him, we've yelled at him, we've coddled him—pretty much done everything we can, but he doesn't usually come to family dinners. It's just too hard for him. I keep hoping…"

Wishing she had social graces was such an understatement. She had no idea what to say, faced with Bethanne Clark's pain and worry. "Matt's fine. You know *he's* fine," she blurted.

"Matthew is fine." Bethanne smiled gently. "It wasn't always the case—you know, I should really let Matt tell you about Matt. It's really not my place to talk about him." She winked. "Especially not with him in the other room."

The front door opened and Lara could hear Sheriff Clark's booming voice. She'd seen Emerald County's sheriff on the news and on billboards at election time, but she'd never met him in person.

He entered the kitchen, energy and vitality entering with him. His dark curly hair was exactly like Matt's, but his eyes were a bright, hard blue instead of the warm brown of Matt and his mother.

Bethanne introduced them. "Reid, this is Lara, Matt's partner. Lara, this is Matthew's father, Reid."

Reid Clark closed his large hand around hers. "Well, if there had been such beautiful women in the fire department back when I was choosing a career, I might've been a firefighter, too."

"Nice to meet you, sir." Lara didn't know what to think of Matt's dad. He'd complimented her but managed to subtly insult Matt at the same time.

Matt walked in, a tall burly man with a shock of white hair beside him. "Hey Lara, this is Uncle Owen, Owen Burke. He's not really an uncle. In fact, I don't know why we call him that."

"Because with three strapping boys, your father needed help to keep you out of trouble and toeing the line. Not that it ever helped."

Matt's smile was an easy curve and Lara found herself wishing again that she had that kind of easy confidence outside of work. "Hey, I always kept my toe just on the edge of the line."

"Yeah, the far edge of the danger line. I took you to the emergency room more times when you were a kid, isn't that right, Bethanne?" Owen put an arm around Bethanne and kissed her on the head.

"He's right, Matt. It took all of us to keep you out of harm's way." She crossed to her son and patted him. "Fortunately, we did a good job and you turned out fine."

Matt's father clapped Owen on the shoulder. "Since you raised him, we'll blame you for the fact that he's a firefighter and not a cop."

All motion in the room stopped.

Bethanne bustled into the deficit. "Dinner's ready. Go get a plate off the dining room table and come serve yourselves. And, Matt, tell Marcus if he doesn't turn off that video game, it's mine for a month."

"Yes, ma'am." Matt left the room and Lara watched the trio of Owen, Bethanne and Reid make their way into the dining room.

She was beginning to see why Matt sometimes got that look on his face when she talked about his perfect family. Maybe nothing was as perfect as it appeared.

For Matt, the dinner with Lara and his family went by both too fast and not fast enough. Watching her interact with his mom and Marcus gave him a vague ache in the middle of his chest.

Marcus conned Lara into a game of Guitar Hero and she stood in front of the TV in the family room, her hip cocked, the guitar strap over her shoulder. As the song ended, she lifted her guitar with a flourish. "Ha! I rock!"

His thirteen-year-old brother smirked at her. "Yeah, on medium. Let's see you try to beat this one on expert."

She pushed him and he fell back on the sofa beside her, laughing. "Not a chance. I concede the victory."

"I guess so. You stink."

"Marcus." Bethanne said it gently, but the warning tone in her voice was unmistakable.

"She does, Mom. You always say I should tell the truth."

Matt laughed. "He's got you there, Mom."

"He should go study his vocabulary words before I forget how fond I am of him." Bethanne sipped at her coffee, calm and cool.

Marcus stood and grabbed his backpack off the floor. "Glad to know my company is appreciated."

Matt surged to his feet and grabbed Marcus in a hug. "We appreciate you. We appreciate when you leave the room."

"'Night, Marcus." Lara stood and placed the guitar gently in its place by the TV.

"Night, Ms. Lara. Come back and play again soon. It was fun beating your brains out." His mother cleared her throat. "I'm going, I'm going."

Matt flopped back on the couch beside Lara. "He's adorable, isn't he?"

She laughed. "Actually, he is, but don't tell him I said that. I don't think any thirteen-year-old wants to hear that they're adorable."

"No, he'd rather hear that he's tough or manly. Or, wow, Marcus, is that hair growing on your chin?"

Lara laughed as Matt's mom acted shocked. "It's okay, Bethanne. I live with a bunch of guys most of the time. They're better now, but the first six months I worked here, they tried everything they could think of to gross me out. Obviously, it didn't work."

"Little boys." Bethanne shook her head.

Matt was pretty sure that his mom was the only person who could get away with calling J.T. and Santos little boys—except maybe for their own moms. "What're Dad and Owen doing holed up back there in the office?"

Even as he spoke, his father's deep voice could be heard coming closer. "I appreciate the donation, Owen. I couldn't keep doing what I'm doing without the support of my old friends."

Owen Burke's voice followed. "You know it's my pleasure to support you as sheriff. We need people like you in charge."

Matt rose to meet them at the door. "Uncle Owen, glad we got to see you tonight."

Owen was a large bear of a man with white hair now, but it had been the blond hair and blue eyes that had made him a favorite of the girls back in his college days with Matt's father. Even after the kids came, Owen had been a fixture at their family events, a favorite uncle to Matt, always bestowing the best gifts, coveted concert tickets or the hottest new electronics.

He clasped his arms around Matt's shoulders. "You, my boy, used to be such a runt. I'm glad to know you're strong enough to haul me out of a burning building."

Matt grimaced. "Yeah, well, you keep letting my mother feed you lasagna and it'll take me and Lara both to carry you out."

With a belly laugh, Owen turned to Lara. "You back this boy up, then?"

Lara flushed pink. "Well, it's a mutual effort, sir."

"He's a lucky man." Owen kissed Bethanne on the mouth. "Thanks for dinner, love. When you get ready to kick Reid out, you give me a call."

Bethanne gave him a friendly shove. "You've been saying that for thirty years, you old coot. Go on with you."

"G'night, everyone."

After the chorus of good-nights, Lara turned to Matt's mom. "Thanks so much for inviting me for dinner, Bethanne. I enjoyed meeting your family. Mr. Clark, it was a pleasure meeting you."

"You, too, Lara. I'm sorry about your house

being broken into. Let me know if there's anything I can do to help."

"Yes, sir, I will. Thank you." She had her keys in her hand. "Matt, before you say anything, I've decided to go to the station and spend the night. I'll be surrounded. It'll be fine.

"That sounds like a fine idea, Lara. And you can call me or Bethanne anytime if you need anything." Matt's dad patted her back and walked toward the kitchen.

"Let me know when you get there. Okay? There've been too many crazy coincidences lately." He slid his hand down her arm to her fingers. "Be careful."

"I will." Lara hesitated, then quickly squeezed his hand and stepped away. "Thanks for everything today."

"Anytime." Matt watched at the door as Lara made it into her car and gave him the thumbs-up. As she drove away, he pulled his own keys out of his pocket.

His dad had relaxed into his favorite leather chair with a cup of coffee and the remote control. He'd been kind to Lara. He was a good guy. Everyone thought so. Matt had worshipped him as a kid. Loved him now.

"Matt, what's this I hear about you going to work for the SBPD?"

"They've asked me to work with their investigators on arson cases and suspicious fires, like the one we're working on now. Basically, if we go through with it, I'll be a firefighter and a cop."

His dad's belly laugh filled the room. "Are they going to let you carry a gun?"

Matt crossed his arms. He wouldn't take the bait. Or maybe he would. "I've been to the FDLE school for law enforcement training, just like most of your deputies."

"I know you're qualified to carry a firearm. I taught you myself, didn't I?" His dad's eyes were on the baseball game.

"Yes, sir, you did." Matt gritted his teeth, just wanting to leave. Why had he ever thought that he'd get his dad's approval by training to be a cop? "I have to go. It's going to be dark soon and I need to get home."

"Fine, fine. I'm sure I'll hear about your case in my interdepartmental meetings tomorrow anyway."

Matt forced himself not to respond in anger. "I'm sure you will, Dad." He found his mom in the kitchen. "Thanks for dinner, Mom. You're a great cook."

His mom laughed and swatted him with the dish towel. "I *am*. You make sure you take care of Lara, Matt. She's going through a lot—and regardless of what else she is to you, she's your partner and your friend."

"I know, and I will." Matt kissed his mother on the cheek. Their family had always gone to church and he never doubted their faith, but his mother was the one who taught him to pray, who taught him to lean on the Lord when he was feeling troubled. She was a strong woman.

Like Lara. He just hoped Lara could find faith when she needed it because it seemed like everywhere she turned, there was trouble.

TEN

Lara took her time driving down the beach road after leaving Matt's parents' house. Late summer evening, the setting sun painting the ocean red, the clouds parting to allow rays of golden color to spear the sky. She wanted to stop by the hospital to check on Emmy and on her mom. She'd called earlier to make sure Ava knew not to go home, but seeing her face and making sure she was holding up every day was important for both of them.

Turning off the beach road, she made the short run to the local hospital. During visiting hours, cars crowded the small parking lots. After a few fruitless circles, she realized that she would have to park in the parking deck. She drove through, slowing down around the corners.

There were only a few people walking around in the concrete structure, but as she rounded one of the corners, the door to one of the storage units opened. Two men were standing in the room and another was outside in the parking lot.

She eased her foot on the brake. One of the men in profile looked really familiar. He turned his head. She caught her breath. It was the man who'd been lurking around the fire scene. The one who'd followed her home.

Lara swallowed hard, her blood chilling in her veins, time slowing to a crawl. As she watched, he spoke to the other man, who looked out at her car. Icy-blue eyes met hers. With her stomach churning, she slammed the car in gear and pushed the accelerator.

Baby J's ever-present bodyguard stepped out in front of her car. She didn't stop.

He leaped to the side as she sped toward the exit ramp, the visit to her family pushed to the side. Her only objective now: getting out of the parking garage.

She'd seen Baby J, the drug dealer, having a meeting with the man from the explosion. A man he supposedly didn't know. A man who knew where she lived.

And Baby J had most certainly recognized her. Her hands were trembling against the steering wheel. She gripped it tighter.

She had to get to Matt. Had to tell him that Baby J was involved in this case, whether he admitted it or not. It was perfectly clear. The reason he'd known where to find her sister was that he'd been involved.

That bodyguard was one serious individual. J was a drug dealer.

The black-haired man was the wild card. And her life was on the line.

Matt was having a tea party on the front steps with the neighbor girls when Lara jerked to a stop in front of his house. Their mom had had to make a last-minute run to the grocery store. Tabitha and Shandy were having tea and cookies—Matt was having chips and salsa.

Lara slammed the door of her car and started across the yard. Even though sunset came late in the summer, darkness had fallen. Matt had the porch lights on—and two portable battery lanterns, one for each girl. For obvious reasons, the twins weren't allowed in his house.

He couldn't see Lara clearly, but she didn't look happy. He'd only parted ways with her a few minutes earlier. What could've happened that would put that look on her face? "Hey. Something going on with Emmy?"

"Not really. I do need to talk to you, though."

She looked over at the girls. "Maybe in a few minutes."

He moved to the side to make room on the top stair for Lara. "Hey, guys, this is my partner, Miss Lara. Think she can join the tea party?"

Lara's cough sounded suspiciously like a laugh, but when he shot a look at her, she was smiling at the girls, who immediately poured her a plastic cup of tea. She sipped it, then looked over at him. "You're not having tea?"

"Pshh. No way. Tea is for girls. I'm having chips and salsa." He lifted a chip and crunched it.

"Manly." She grinned.

"I thought so." Matt reached to right Tabitha's teacup just before it tipped over. "Here, Tab, drink up before it falls over and becomes ant food."

She giggled, then jumped and ran as her mom pulled in the driveway next door. Her sister was right behind her. "Mommy, Mr. Matt made us a tea party."

His neighbor, Alisha, still in her work scrubs and tennis shoes, walked toward them. "That was nice of Mr. Matt. You need to tell him thank-you and pick up your mess, please."

Four little arms clung to his neck. Shandy

placed a sticky kiss on his cheek. "Thanks, Mr. Matt. Love you."

"I love you too, monkey." He stumbled to his feet with a five-year-old girl clamped under each arm. They squealed as he swung them around.

"Okay, enough. I'll never get them to sleep." Alisha laughed and held out a hand to Lara. "Hi, I'm Alisha, Matt's neighbor."

"Lara, Matt's partner."

"Firefighter? That's cool." Alisha turned to the girls. "Head for the house, munchkins. Time for a bath."

She followed them across the yard, calling back to Matt. "Thanks, Matt. I owe you for the rescue."

"No sweat. See you tomorrow." Matt picked up the blanket the girls had been sitting on and shook the crumbs into the grass. "Come on, spill it."

"What?" Lara turned toward Alisha's duplex, the one attached to Matt's, and watched her corral the girls inside. "You know, you're really good with them—a total natural."

"I know, who woulda thought? But they're fun and I really don't watch them that much."

"When did you start helping out with them?"

"A couple of years ago. They would've been, I guess, three?" He patted the step beside him, done with the conversational run-around. "Come on, sit. Talk."

She dropped to the step beside him. "I think Emmy needs protection."

The little girls next door trying to get out of a bath, the dog barking two doors down. The coach down the street mowing his yard at night to escape the heat. All of it dissipated as he focused on what Lara was saying.

"I went to the hospital to visit her and make sure my mom was okay." She paused to look at him.

"Yeah. I can understand why you would do that after what happened today." She was supposed to go directly to the fire station, but if he'd been in her place, he would've gone to the hospital first, too. "Go on."

"I saw Baby J in the parking garage. But that's not what was weird. Matt, he was meeting with the man I saw at the fire scene. The one you saw driving by my house." Even now, thinking back, her palms began to sweat.

"Are you sure?"

"As sure as I can be." She picked at an invisible piece of lint on her jeans, clearly uneasy.

Matt jumped to his feet and took four steps

into the yard before turning back to Lara. The porch light glinted gold on her blond hair. Even in jeans and a shirt, she was so pretty.

"Okay, so Baby J. I really wanted to believe he wasn't involved in this—that he just heard where she was. But." Matt paced toward the driveway, pent-up energy making him restless. "Wait—you said you saw them. Did they see you?"

She sighed. "Yeah. I'm pretty sure Baby J recognized me. And the bodyguard, he definitely recognized me."

"That's not good. All right, here's what we'll do. Let's call Cruse Conyers and see if he can get a uniformed officer up to Emmy's floor to sit outside her door." He paused. "Now you. Your house has been broken into. I think it's obvious that someone is associating you with this case. You need to go straight to the station house if that's where you want to stay."

She didn't move, just sat there staring into the street. "Matt, I'm scared. I don't want to be involved in this."

Wrapping an arm around her shoulders, he pulled her to his chest, her honesty shaking him, stunning him. He leaned his head to touch hers. "I know, but we're going to get the people behind this. The more evidence we find, the closer we get."

She leaned in, fitting herself in the curve of his arm. The fact that she'd trusted him with this meant something. Man, he wished things could be different. That they could erase their past and just be two people who became friends, maybe turning into something more.

It wasn't who they were. As much as he wanted it, he wasn't sure Lara would ever let it be more.

And it was his loss.

"I should go."

"Yeah, you probably should." He didn't move.

She stood, but her eyes met his and held. "Thanks, for being a friend even though I haven't been acting like one."

"No need to go there, Bump. We've all got things that trip us up occasionally. It'll take time to work through it and I've got plenty of that."

Her lips parted. She still didn't move toward the car. Could it be that she didn't want to go as badly as he wanted her to stay?

Pulling her to him, he held her close. He could feel her breathe, feel her heartbeat even with his, her hair brushing his chin.

Difficult as it was, he had to let her go. "I'll

call Conyers and get him to post someone outside Emmy's room. And I'll walk you to your car, but you have to promise you're going straight to the station."

"I promise." She slid into the driver's seat, closed the door and rolled the window down. "You're something else, you know that, Clark?"

"Yeah, yeah, get out of here. It's still your day to cook tomorrow."

He heard her laugh as she drove away. His smile faded. She was in danger. He didn't know why or who exactly, but he would find out. And he would neutralize the threat.

Matt picked up the quilt and the chips and salsa plate and opened the door to his house. He hadn't left any lights on and the whole place was dark and quiet, but...the sense of space didn't feel right. He wasn't alone.

Silently, Matt laid the armload of stuff down by the door of his duplex. After the break-in at Lara's he wasn't taking any chances. He slid open a drawer on the antique sideboard in his front hall. His weapon in hand, he thumbed off the safety.

Eyes adjusted to the dark, he braced the handgun and whipped around the corner, his pulse pounding in his ears. His living room was empty. Easing down the hall, he cleared first one bedroom then another, then his office.

The kitchen was the only room left.

He crept down the hall, careful not to step on the creaky spots in the wood floor, and stepped over the threshold.

"You can put that away, little brother, it's just me." Tyler sat in the shadows, his back against the wall.

His brother was dressed in sloppy jeans, a long black T-shirt and a black hoodie. A pistol lay on the table beside him in the dark.

"Why did you come here, Tyler?" Matt tucked his service weapon into the waistband of his jeans at the small of his back.

"I can't come by to see my baby brother?"

Matt reached for the light switch, but Tyler's voice, harsh and direct, cut him off. "Don't turn on the light."

"Fine." Questions cartwheeling through his mind, Matt faced his brother. "Forget coming to see me—it'd be nice if you'd go see Mom now and then. It's killing her not knowing where you are. Even Ethan goes to dinner once a month. You know how hard that is for him. Oh wait, maybe you don't. You missed the funeral."

"I can't go home."

"Whatever. You've always done exactly what

you wanted to do anyway." Matt leaned against the door frame, determined not to let Tyler get to him.

Tyler nodded slowly and raised his lanky body from the chair and wandered the room, straightening things. A picture frame here, a dish towel there. Everything perfectly in its place. Everything perfect. Tyler had always been that way.

Matt closed his eyes. He was beyond those old inadequacies, fighting for his dad's attention. When he opened them again, his brother was leaned against the sink, his arm crossed over his chest. "What are you really here for, Ty?"

"To tell you to back off. You're in over your head." Tyler's stance was lazy. The words were not.

"You've got to be kidding me." Matt's breath burst out. "It's been a long time since you've had the right to tell me what to do. What do you know about what I'm doing, anyway?"

"You're a firefighter, Matt, not a cop, not an agent. You're not prepared to go up against guys like this." Tyler turned around and leaned against the counter, crossing his arms, one of which sported a dragon tattoo on the biceps.

"I'm a firefighter *and* a cop." He answered

before he realized that Tyler hadn't answered his question.

Tyler laughed. "You think four weeks of training at the FDLE school will prepare you for the Diablo Brotherhood?"

"It doesn't matter. I'm already involved." The weight of his older brother's lack of faith in him stung. And then the words sunk in. Tyler knew more about this case than he did. "What about the Diablo Brotherhood?"

"Stay away from them, Matt. They're ruthless. You don't know them."

"And *you* do?"

"I've been one of them for the last eighteen months." Tyler's voice was low, guttural. And bleak.

Matt halted midstep. Now *that* revelation was unexpected. Cruse Conyers's words came back to him. The DEA had a man on the inside. And maybe it finally made sense why Tyler had been away so long. "Undercover?"

Tyler scratched the stubble on his chin. "I can't talk about it."

Ah, man. "I can't believe you would do that, not to Mom, not after Ethan."

"It's my job, Matt."

"When are you going to tell them?" Matt

stopped pacing and dropped into the chair Tyler had vacated.

"I'm not. You know how this works. I shouldn't be here now."

"I also know Mom and that not knowing where you are or if you're even alive is tearing her up." When Tyler didn't speak, Matt's mind turned circles around this new information. And like lightning he made the connection. "It was you I saw at that house."

Tyler's eyes bored into Matt's, his jaw set. Matt stared right back. He hadn't been intimidated by his brother in years, since about the time he lost respect for him.

"That girl was bad news, a major addict. She was hanging with one of the Brothers."

"She's my partner's sister. She nearly died from this new drug on the street." He let his disgust show on his face. "What happened to you?"

Tyler stopped, took a breath. "You need to be careful, Matt. They're looking for her and they'll find her eventually."

Matt ignored the statement hanging in the air, choosing to file it away for later, instead focusing on what his brother was doing with that group of criminals. "Tyler, that drug is poison. A sixteen-year-old girl died right in front of me the other day. If you can help, you have to help."

"I'll do what I can. When I can. This case is building to a head faster than either one of us could've predicted. There's so much pressure on them that I'm not sure we can contain it. I have to find out who's pulling the strings on the Brothers before it all blows up in our face." Tyler started for the door but turned back. "I'm sorry about your partner's sister. Is she going to be okay?"

"Yes, probably." Matt stared into Tyler's eyes, black in the dark kitchen. "Are you?"

The corner of Tyler's mouth lifted, not even a smile. "I hope so. I left my cell number on the table. Text me if you have to get in touch with me. And do me a favor. Don't tell Mom you saw me."

Despite his frustration, he was worried about his brother. "Tyler…"

"Be careful, Matt. These guys are in business to make money. And they are deadly serious."

ELEVEN

Matt sat beside Emmy's bed the next morning, his hands folded in front of him. He didn't really remember learning how to pray. It seemed that it had always been a part of his life, a part of who he was. Maybe the most crucial part. Even in his darkest days, he always prayed.

Some of those were reckless demands. Some were heartfelt pleas that God would show up because Matt needed Him desperately. His family life hadn't been anything close to the perfect life Lara imagined it to be. Far from it.

But his mother's faith? Now that was something to hang on to. And somewhere along the way it had become his.

Emmy had been downgraded from critical to serious this morning and moved onto the floor from ICU. She was still being monitored closely. There were six single-serving cereal boxes of kiddie cereal lined up on the window sill. He could tell Lara had been to see Emmy already this morning.

Emmy stirred, restless and uncomfortable, the effects of detox. So Matt prayed. She could find physical healing here, but it was going to take more than just a physical detox to heal the hurt that caused her to keep going to drugs.

As he watched, she opened her eyes. Hazel eyes that reminded him of Lara. Her gaze bounced around the sterile white room, trying to place where she was, until it rested on him. He could see her trying to figure out why he was there.

"You're a cop?" She licked dry, cracked lips.

"Firefighter. I'm Matt." Matt walked to her tray table and poured her a cup of water. He slid the tray closer to her, instinctively knowing that she wouldn't want him close enough to touch her.

She took one tiny sip and struggled to swallow it. "You know my sister?"

He nodded.

"Bet she loves that you're here." Her tone, dry as dust, tested him out.

He sat back in the seat he'd just vacated. Actually, Lara had no idea he was there. And while he was pretty sure she wouldn't have wanted him to come this morning, after hearing that his brother knew she was there, he felt like he needed to. "What do you mean, Emmy?"

"She wouldn't want you anywhere near me. I'm such a mess." Her words were frank and direct, but she looked away, fingering the stiff white hospital sheet.

"You are that." He smiled. "But you're on your way to getting better. Did you see Ben yet?"

"I don't want to see him." Her lips trembled, belying her words. She wanted to be tough, but she couldn't quite pull it off.

"He was so happy when I told him that we found you. That man loves you." The raw emotions were so close to the surface that Matt could see every one as it crossed her face. He knew what it felt like to feel worthless, to try to prove to everyone that you were worth saving and then mess up again. To always be hurting the ones you love the most.

Emmy turned away, her throat working. "You don't know what you're talking about. Maybe Ben cared about me before, but he couldn't love me now. Look at me."

"Ben loves you, Emmy." His heart broke for this precious girl, who couldn't see that she was beautiful simply because God made her. He knew it was hard. He'd been there. "But there is Someone who loves you more, more than you can even imagine."

He kept his voice quiet, but he tried to put every bit of the certainty he knew into it.

"If you're talking about God, there's no way that God would want me. I'm so gross."

"It doesn't matter where you've been or how many times you walk away, God wants you to come to Him. He can give you peace. He can save you, Emmy, even from this." Hadn't Matt had to learn that it didn't matter what anyone else thought of him? Only God.

Tears streamed down her face. "I can't beat this. I've tried. I believe in God. I went to church."

"Everybody falls down sometimes—everyone makes mistakes. You can beat this, Emmy. There's nothing you can't do with Him on your side. You have Lara and Ben to support you. And you have that gorgeous baby girl who needs a mommy." Sometimes it just took speaking the truth over and over and over again. She'd been telling herself the damaging words for so many years. She needed to hear healing words, not the ones she'd been telling herself all her life.

She ran the tips of her fingers over her

damaged lips, her voice a strangled whisper. "Look at me. I'm so ugly. How could anyone want me?"

"Your disease is ugly. Emmy, *you* are beautiful."

Behind him the door slammed against the wall. He caught just a glimpse of Lara's blond hair as she bolted out the door and down the hall. Great.

But he couldn't think about that now. He pulled his chair closer to the bed and leaned toward Emmy, wanting her to see. "Listen to me. I've been where you are. Not with drugs, but with other stuff just as bad. I isolated myself from my family because I thought they'd be better off without me. I told myself that I was better off making my own way." He let that sink in for a second. "I isolated myself from God because I thought He couldn't possibly want me. Use me. But I was wrong. And so are you."

Her hands were quiet on the sheet, and though her quivering lip was still clenched tightly between her teeth, he could tell she was thinking about it. She wanted to believe that there was another way. "We'll support you for as long as you need it, Emmy. All you have to do is want to get better."

She grabbed a tissue off the tray table in front

of her and mopped her nose. In her eyes, he could see just the beginning of clarity. "I want it. I want it more than anything."

"Okay." He smiled. "We can work with that. Do you mind if I—"

"Please go after her. I'm not going anywhere." A hint of a smile crossed Emmy's ravaged face.

Matt shot out the door and down the hall to the stairs. Outside he stopped, the heat a slap in the face after the cold, sterile environment of the hospital. Where would she go?

Not home. He knew her well enough to know she wouldn't risk driving when she was that upset. Maybe to the garden.

He turned to the left and took the walkway through the trees into the courtyard. Lara was sitting on a bench tucked into the back corner, her flip-flops kicked off into the grass beside her.

Slowly he walked toward her. "Hey."

She looked up and met his eyes with hers. In them, he could see such pain, he felt it inside, a deep ache. She gestured at the bench and scooted to the side to make room for him to sit down.

"Wanna tell me what happened up there?"

She looked at her feet, digging her toes into

the soft, cool grass. "I'm not even sure. I can't—
Did you mean what you said?"

"I don't know which part you're talking about,
but you know me, Lara. Do I usually say things
I don't mean?" He lifted his hands.

"She's so sick, so damaged. Everything she
touches has always—" She cut herself off.
"Everything is falling apart, Matt. I've tried so
hard to keep it together and I just can't."

"Maybe that's the trouble. You can't hold it
together on your own. You're so independent,
Lara. I know with all you've had to deal with in
your life that you had to be. But at some point,
you just have to trust that Someone stronger
than you is going to help you hold on."

"I know God is there. I do. Sometimes it's
just really hard to hear Him." Her bottom lip
trembled and she immediately bit down on it.
She hated to show emotion. Despite everything
they'd been through, opening herself up to him
was still so hard for her. He knew it, but it was
too important to let it go now.

"Lara, everybody has stuff in their life. A
past. I do. I ran with a crowd whose favorite
pastime was getting drunk and stealing cars.
I thought that I couldn't live up to what my
parents wanted for me, so I was going to do

everything I could to be the opposite of that." He could see the shock in her eyes.

She shook her head, not buying into it. "You were just a kid."

"Yeah? I was a kid who got picked up by the cops and nearly went to jail. If it hadn't been for Pastor Jake, I would have. He was a firefighter then and working with the youth group at the church." Matt laughed. "He started coming by my house every Saturday morning and picking me up to go lift weights. He talked to me about God and about being a firefighter."

"Is Jake that much older than you are?" She leaned forward, getting into the story enough to forget that she was upset with him.

"Nah. He just saw a train wreck about to happen. Every Friday night, I told myself I wouldn't go with him the next day. Every Saturday morning, I was up at the crack of dawn, waiting for him. He saved my life."

Lara firmed her still-trembling lips. "There was no one there for Emmy."

"Aw, hon, that's not true. You were always there for her."

She stood and paced to the edge of the grassy clearing and turned back to face him. "I just realized you pretty much know everything there is to know about me now. You know my mother's sick and my sister's a drug addict and you know just how close I am to the edge." Her hands shook as she pushed her bangs out of her face.

"And yet, here I am."

"That's what I don't understand." She sent him a helpless look. "Why are you still here?"

He looked up into the sky, took a deep breath and blew it out. "Seriously, Lara, are you really that dense? Can you *really* not figure it out?"

Putting her hand on his arm, she slid it around to cup his biceps. "We're more than coworkers. We're friends. I know that now, but I've never had a friend, not like you."

He laughed under his breath. "Yeah, okay, we're friends, I'll give you that."

"I don't understand."

She was killing him. And he had to let her find her own way. "I know you don't. Right now, all you need to know is that it doesn't matter to me what your family does or doesn't do or whether they have two brain cells to rub together. I care about *you*."

Then she looked at him with that bewildered expression, and in his mind he simply gave up the fight. He slid his hand into the softness of her hair at the base of her neck and drew her face close to his.

He didn't kiss her, just stayed there a breath away. The pulse in her neck raced under his fingertips. The corners of his lips turned up as he eased forward ever so slightly and brushed his lips over hers.

A soft breath escaped her lips, his name.

When she reached to tangle her hand in his T-shirt, his lips teased over hers again. He drew back, his heart pounding in his chest.

"I've wanted to do this for such a long time," he murmured against her lips.

This time it was Lara that pulled him in. She tasted him tentatively. Her eyes drifted closed.

She pushed him away and jumped to her feet. "What am I doing? We *work* together. You're my partner. We— Matt, we can't do this."

Matt didn't move, couldn't. He just stood at the edge of the courtyard, his arms at his sides. He'd known this would happen, but he'd gone there anyway. He had no one to blame but himself.

"I have to go." She took three steps toward the building and turned back, her fingertips at her lips. She stared at him for a long moment.

He still didn't say anything. He wasn't going to convince her. She had to come around to this on her own or not at all. His deepest fear was that he would scare her away and that in pushing him away she'd be pushing God further away, too.

"I'm sorry. I just can't risk losing the only thing that makes sense in my life." Lara walked away again, this time not looking back.

Matt stood and watched her make it safely into the building before digging his car keys out of his pocket and blowing out a frustrated breath. "Yeah, that went well."

Lara dumped stew meat into the slow cooker. A lot of stew meat. Firefighters were a hungry bunch. And they tended to eat more than once if they got called out. The growling sounds of a racing video game came from the room next door, interspersed with frequent yells from the "drivers."

She scraped a few cans of condensed cream of mushroom soup and added a packet of French onion soup powder.

J.T. sauntered into the kitchen and reached around her to pluck a piece of bell pepper. He leaned back against the counter and crossed his legs. "Mmm, stew. I think I'll make tacos when it's my turn."

"You always make tacos, J.T." She finished chopping the onions and added them to the mix in the cooker. "What are you doing in here? Dinner won't be ready for hours."

"I lost the first round of Mario Kart, so I got kicked out. Blankenship is Princess Peach and he's beating the brains out of everyone. Speaking of losing, have you been on your date with Matt yet?"

Lara's hands jerked as she sliced the peppers, just a slight hiccup, nothing noticeable. She didn't look at J.T. "I went to dinner at his parents' house."

"That doesn't count. *I've* been to dinner at his parents' house."

Santos came in and started searching the cabinets. "Can't believe Blankenship is winning with Peach. Wearing a dress. Ridiculous."

J.T. called out to Santos, "Lara thinks that going to dinner at Matt's house counts as fulfilling the dare."

Santos opened a bag of chips and sat at the kitchen table, propping one booted foot on the other chair. "No way, it doesn't count. *I've* been to dinner at Matt's parents' house. You ready to forfeit?"

She was beginning to think she was the only one who hadn't been to dinner at Matt's family's home until now. Santos's words sunk in. *Forfeit?* Never.

Lara ground pepper over the top of the stew, replaced the top and slid it to the back of the counter to cook. She turned to face them. "I will never back out on a dare. So you can stop planning whatever it is you're planning for when I don't complete it."

Santos grinned, white teeth flashing in dusky skin. His sooty black hair was always falling forward into his eyes. He pushed it back with an unconscious gesture. "Does that mean you're not going to have to clean the toilets for a month?"

Lara shuddered. "That's cruel and unusual punishment. I'm assuming you have bathroom duty this week?"

When his smile only grew wider, she tapped him on the head with her knuckles. "Forget it. You get no satisfaction here."

J.T. reached into Miguel's bag of chips. "Don't forget we require proof. And it has to be a date."

She pointed her wooden spoon at him. "*You* are relentless. I've got it."

When the alarm tones sounded, they pushed to their feet in unison, jogging into the truck bay. J.T. poked Lara. "Relentlessness is a good trait for a firefighter."

"Yeah, yeah." In practiced motions, Lara

pulled on turnout gear. She met Matt sliding into the seat of the rig. "Accident with injury?"

"Out on the highway. There's a kid involved."

The ride to the site passed in a blur of multiple sirens, horns and lights. She tried to remember on every run that, although these things were commonplace to her, they meant a crisis situation for the person who needed them. And when someone's child was hurt, the stress level increased ten-fold.

Santos braked the rig. As they piled out into the baking midday sun, she realized they'd be needing the extrication gear. The compact car was a mangled mess. The truck that hit it—a Ford F-150, with its much heavier body—had fared only slightly better.

Todd was assessing the driver of the truck, whose face was bleeding, while Daniel was at the car with the mother and child. She could hear the child screaming from where she was. He waved Lara over. "Can you check on Mom? I need to try to get the little one out as soon as possible. He was in a seat, but..."

"Got it." On the driver's side, she tried the door, which wouldn't open. She could see the mom through the broken window, but the young woman wasn't moving. The window was partially gone but not enough to reach in. With her gloves, she quickly pulled out the remaining glass. As she did, the woman roused, moaning. And whoa, the alcohol fumes slapped her in the face. That was a lot of alcohol before noon.

"Hey, there. I'm Lara. I'm with the fire department. We're going to get you out of there. Okay?"

"Baby? My baby?" The mom still hadn't opened her eyes, but she lifted her hand in a reaching motion.

"He's going to be just fine. He was in his seat and we're getting him out now."

The beach traffic had backed up on the highway and impatient drivers honked their horns, rubbernecking to see what had happened.

Lara brushed glass off the young woman's shoulders and took her pulse. "What's your name?"

The woman's eyelids wrinkled as she thought and she moaned again, her lips moving but no sound coming out. Finally, Lara heard, "Shelly."

"Okay, Shelly, can you tell me what hurts?" She lifted Shelly's eyelids one at a time to check her pupils. Equal and reactive.

"Everything hurts." Yeah, that made sense

after the kind of wreck she'd just had, but specifics were better.

Lara grabbed a cervical collar from the kit Daniel had left on the ground by the car. She wrapped it around Shelly's neck, stabilizing it. "This is just to protect your neck okay, Shelly? Can you tell me what you had to drink today?"

The young woman's eyes rolled open. "Nothing."

She hollered over the noise of traffic to Daniel. "Stethoscope?"

He tossed it to her and she put it on, listening for clear breath sounds. Which they were. Lara pulled the stethoscope off and draped it around her neck.

"Shelly, we can't give you any pain meds unless we know how much you've had to drink." She wrapped the blood-pressure cuff around the woman's arm and pumped it.

The victim licked her lips, her reactions slow and deliberate. "May-Maybe one or two beers."

They could assume three or four. And her blood pressure was really low.

"Okay, Shelly, can you tell me what hurts the worst?"

"Legs. Stomach." Shelly's head rolled to the side and she moaned again. "Please help me."

"Okay, hon. We're gonna get you out just as quick as we can." Shelly's legs were trapped under the collapsed dash, but Lara reached in with her left hand to palpate the abdomen. *Oh, boy.*

She pulled the walkie-talkie clipped to her coat closer to her mouth. "Matt, we need to get her out of the car now. Get LifeFlight on the radio. Her belly is hot and rigid."

"Cops called 'em. They're already on the way. Let's get her out of there." Matt appeared behind her holding the fifty-pound spreader in his hands like a child's toy. The spreader would be used to pop the hinges of the ruined door and get their injured patient out quickly. J.T. and Santos had the backboard on the ground and were standing by, ready to help move her to the helicopter.

She glanced back at Todd. The driver of the Ford had obviously been cut up pretty badly. Todd had him on the ground and was still working to contain the bleeding.

While Matt worked to get Shelly out of the vehicle, Lara rounded the car to where Daniel was assessing the little boy, who was around two years old. His screams nearly drowned out the sound of Matt's hydraulic tool.

"Hey, buddy. That noise is really loud, isn't it? I bet you're wondering where your mom is." She walked to the car and looked in as Matt and Santos popped the door from the other side. Not bad. Maybe five minutes on scene and they were ready to get her out and on her way. In the distance, she heard the thumping of chopper blades. Perfect timing. LifeFlight would land right behind them on the highway.

She looked into the backseat. All over the floor were party items. Plates and cups and balloons. All with the number two on them. A cake had upended in the box and was smashed on the floorboard behind the driver's seat.

A birthday party. Lara swallowed hard.

There on the backseat of the car was a tattered piece of a blanket. She shook it to make sure there were no pieces of glass stuck to it and crouched down in front of the little boy. "Here you go, handsome. Just for you."

He pulled it close, stuck his thumb in his mouth and gave Daniel a dirty look. Daniel laughed. "He's all set. That little cut on his head is the worst of it. They'll probably CT him at the hospital, but he looks good. Can you get him out while I help with the mom?"

"Her name is Shelly. She's diaphoretic, her pulse is 120 and thready, respirations shallow and irregular, blood pressure 60/40. Belly hot and distended. She admits to drinking two beers before driving." She lifted the little one into her arms. His breath came in jerks after his long crying bout, his eyelashes stuck together in spikey points. He looked at her with suspicion, but he didn't cry again.

One of the cops on the scene brought over a diaper bag. "This was in the car."

"Thanks." She hooked the strap over her shoulder and then flipped the tag up where she could read it. "Let's see who you are—Brody. Cute. And you are two years old today."

She blew out the breath that wanted to catch in her throat and hitched him higher on her hip. "Okay, birthday boy. You ready to go for a ride in the ambulance?"

He blinked big blue eyes, but the thumb remained in his mouth as she walked him over to the ambulance and sat on the bumper.

Todd had joined Daniel, and the two of them had Brody's mom on the bright orange backboard, strapping her in for the ride to the regional medical center's trauma unit. From what Lara could see, the mom was still conscious, talking. While she watched, Todd dropped a line for an

IV. Fluids were crucial if they wanted to keep her alive until they got her to the hospital.

Police officers, including Joe Sheehan, had managed to stop traffic going both directions as the helicopter gently touched down. Within seconds, the medic was out and running for them. He lifted one side of the backboard and as they carried her to the helicopter, Lara could see Daniel leaning over her, lips moving, reporting her condition to the paramedic who would fly with her to the hospital.

They slid Shelly into the helicopter and Daniel climbed on board with the LifeFlight paramedic. Within seconds, it lifted off the ground.

Another ambulance arrived on scene to take the driver of the truck to the hospital as the wreckers arrived to move the cars from the highway. Todd passed the driver over to the EMTs on the arriving ambulance and came to check out the baby. "How's he holding up?"

"Fine. There's a lot of stuff to look at, but it has to be confusing and scary for him." She patted the little boy's back.

Todd clicked his penlight on and checked the baby's pupils again. "So far, so good. You up for a ride?"

"Absolutely. Just let me tell Matt that I'm riding back with you guys."

Todd turned and yelled to Matt. "Lara's riding along."

Matt gave him a thumbs-up and went back to managing the scene.

Lara climbed in the back of the ambulance with the little boy. Todd slammed the doors behind her and went around to drive. As the siren started with a slow wail, Lara thought about this little boy's mother. Hopefully she would survive what probably started out as a routine trip to the grocery store.

Things changed so fast—in an instant, really. For Emmy, it had been a cup of coffee with a person she thought would be safe. For this little boy, it had been a split-second decision that his mom made, the kind everybody makes a thousand times a day. Go to the store. Don't go to the store. Pull into that opening in traffic. Wait for another one. Answer the cell phone. Let it ring.

And now he didn't have anyone to celebrate his birthday with. Lara knew what that felt like. She'd never had a party. No presents, no cake. No birthday wishes. She'd outgrown the desire—she didn't miss it anymore.

This sweet little fella wouldn't have a birthday this year. And he wouldn't have his mom for a long time.

Things changed. In an instant.

Lara had been waiting to try to have a normal life, and for what? For her mom to stop being bipolar? For her sister to get clean? For herself to feel like she was swimming rather than barely keeping her head above water?

She swayed as the ambulance turned a corner. As the baby whimpered, she pulled him close.

With everything that had been going on, she'd hardly had time to breathe. But did she want to get to the end of her life and have missed what life had to offer? The moments of peace, of fun, were so few, but they were bright spots of living color.

She didn't want to miss them. But thinking about letting go of control after fighting all these years to gain it—just the thought had her insides in more of a tangle than the clump of costume jewelry she had sitting on her dresser at home.

The fact remained. If she wanted to live life, she had to stop being afraid of it. And *that* was easier said than done.

TWELVE

Matt entered the lobby of the hospital. He needed to see Emmy and ask her a few questions. In the morning, her husband, Ben, would take her to rehab, where she would stay for the next four weeks. It would be a tough time for her, but at the end of it, she would have the chance for a new life. Matt hoped she would take it.

The elevator doors opened on the third floor. He exited and walked to Emmy's room, showing ID to the officer sitting outside her door.

He pushed the door open. Lara's sister was dressed in jeans and a pink T-shirt, sitting cross-legged in bed, her eyes clear and her hair combed. "Wow, you look—"

"Sober?" Emmy cracked a smile. "I'd been sober thirteen months and ten days before, well, believe me, I like this better."

"You look fantastic. It's gonna stick." Matt

sat in the chair closest to Emmy's bed. "I need to ask you a few questions."

"Seriously? I thought you were a firefighter." The wary look on her face wasn't good. He didn't want her to think he'd been supporting her because he wanted something from her. He had to take a risk, though. Had to know if she had information that could help them.

"I am a firefighter, but a fire we're investigating has ties to drug manufacturers. We think you may have information that could lead us to them."

She fiddled with the hairbrush in her lap. "I answered questions for the police already. I don't know anything. I'm not involved with this new drug."

"I don't know how you were involved, but you're obviously involved with the Diablo Brotherhood somehow. I read the transcript, but I'd really like to hear the story in your own words. Okay?"

When she slowly nodded her head, he began. "How did you get started doing drugs again? Did school get to be too much for you?"

"No—it was stressful, for sure, but I liked it. I felt like I was finally able to do something with my life." She shrugged it off, a gesture that made Matt so sad.

"That opportunity is going to come again, Emmy. I promise." She nodded without looking at him, her eyes on the single flower arrangement, a small vase of daisies. He hated this, hated asking questions that made her have to rethink the terrible time that she'd been through, but he had to know, had to hear it from her.

"What else did you do with your time?" Matt slid a notebook out of his back pocket and showed it to Emmy. "Will it be okay if I take notes?"

"Sure, I guess. I took care of the baby, took her to the park and stuff. Went to meetings."

"What kind of meetings?" His heart beat a little faster. He made a note to check it out—the meetings could be a place where the Brotherhood targeted recovering addicts like Emmy.

"I go to Faith Community in Fort Walton Beach. It's close to my apartment and they have Celebrate Recovery there. And a nursery." Emmy fingered the seam of her jeans.

"Emmy, what happened?" Matt, his voice as gentle as he could make it, put the notebook aside on the table. "How did you end up in that house with those men?"

Emmy swallowed, the pain of it obviously weighing on her. Their interview wasn't the cause. And getting to the root of all this was the only thing that might possibly help. Knowing the truth was best for both of them.

"One night after my meeting, I was studying at this coffee shop near the college. This guy, I thought I'd seen him at church before, he sat down at the table with me. He bought me a cup of coffee. As soon as I drank it, I knew something wasn't right, but I—I didn't tell anyone. I wanted everything to stay the same. I left and went home to Ben and Charis. Ben's such a good person. He didn't even notice I was juiced."

She buried her chin in her chest, her voice dropping to a whisper. "God help me, the next day I went back. It felt good at first, you know? Addiction tricks you into thinking that you can have a life and drugs, but that's a lie."

She raised her head and met Matt's eyes, hers so much like Lara's that it startled him for a second. "I couldn't stay away once I'd been high again."

"How'd you get from going to the coffee shop to meet this guy to living in that house?"

She chewed her lip. "He sent me to this club on the beach. It was kind of a front. People went there who didn't do drugs, but the people who do drugs know they can get them there, if that makes sense."

"Yeah, it does. Where's the club?"

Her head dropped back on the pillow. "Those guys are really bad. I don't want them to come looking for me."

Matt knew that they probably already were. He squeezed Emmy's hand. "Just a few more questions."

She pressed her lips together. "I don't want anyone else to go through what I did. The club is called Sand Dollar."

Matt's heart began to pound. This could be the break they'd been looking for. That club was here in Sea Breeze. Right on *their* beach.

Matt dug in his pants pocket again, coming up with a few pictures. He laid them on the bed in front of Emmy. One was a mug shot taken from a newspaper article. The other was Baby J. The third was a picture of Tyler.

He pointed to the pictures. "Did you ever see any of these three people?"

Emmy pointed to Baby J. "I've seen him. I don't know what they talked about because they shot me up and made me leave the room when he came to the house. I could hear their voices, though. They were always yelling."

She picked up the newspaper clipping. "This guy is one of the ones who lives in the house.

One of the Diablo Brotherhood. He has the tattoo."

Pointing to the picture of Matt's brother Tyler, Emmy shivered. "Him I know. I never got a name—I think they called him T-bone. He was at the house, kind of like a bodyguard for the main guy."

Matt pulled one more sheet of paper out of his back pocket. "What about this guy? Do you recognize him?"

She began to shake.

"Emmy?" She was looking at the drawing of their suspect, the one he and Lara had seen.

"That's the man who met me at the coffee shop. He's the one who kept bringing me drugs. He's the one who made me do all those things." Tremors vibrated in her voice. She was scared to death. Angry. Probably all of the above. "His name is Alfred Baxter."

"Emmy, do you want to talk about what they did to you?"

Her eyes sought his. He wished he could give her courage, or direction. But at some point, she had to make those decisions on her own.

Emmy's eyes filled and tears spilled over. "I would've done anything for the drug. *Anything.* And they knew it. They used me to run drugs for them." She pointed at J's picture. "To this guy's house. Now that I think about it, he's probably their distributor."

Matt made a mental note. "What else, Emmy?"

"They used me...other ways, too. They would've killed me. It was only a matter of time. If you hadn't found me, I probably would've died that day."

Matt reached for Emmy's other hand. "I'm glad I did find you."

"Me, too." Her smile was trembling, but it was real.

There was a knock at the door and Ben walked in, carrying the baby. When he saw Matt, he shuffled one foot along the terrazzo floor, then looked at Emmy. "I couldn't wait to see you. I hope it's okay that I came early."

"Of course it's okay, Ben." Emmy put her toiletries on the bedside table. "Matt was just giving me the lowdown on everything, and I think they've got it under control. Can I... Do you mind if I..." She twisted the sheet in her fingers.

"You want to hold Charis? She's missed her mommy." Ben handed Emmy the baby and sat on the edge of the bed.

Matt smiled as he saw Emmy nuzzle her baby girl's soft head—raw, unfettered love on her face. She had a long, long road ahead of her, but she had some really good reasons to travel it.

Matt walked to the door and then turned back. "Be strong, Emmy. We're pulling for you."

What a nightmare. Hooked by someone whose only goal was to take advantage of her. She'd become their pawn, their stool and their toy. It made him sick.

But he was going to take them down.

Downstairs in the E.R., Lara sat at the end of the bed in little Brody's room, playing pat-a-cake with the little boy. One of the nurses had blown up a latex glove and Brody squealed as he waved it in the air. Her turnouts were piled in the corner in a chair.

Her shift had ended an hour ago. Brody's mom had been rushed to emergency surgery. The cops were trying to find his dad or a grandma. Someone to take care of him until they could sort out whether his mom would be charged with anything. What a mess.

She heard a throat clear behind her and turned around to find her mom. Ava was wearing a pretty blue capri outfit, almost like sweatpants with a short-sleeved jacket over her tank top.

With her hair in a long ponytail and her wispy bangs, she looked like a teenager.

"I hope it's okay that I came down. I was leaving and one of the nurses told me you were here." Ava's uncertain smile made Lara feel guilty. She'd barely seen her mother since Emmy came into the hospital.

She smiled and scooched over on the bed. "Come meet Brody. Brody, this is my mom."

He raised big blue eyes, full of questions. "Mommy?"

Her heart went out to him. He'd been asking for his mom all afternoon. No matter what she'd done, she was this baby's mommy and he loved her with unwavering devotion. "Mommy's with the doctor, bud. You'll see her soon."

She hoped it was true.

Ava hesitated in the doorway, then brought a plastic grocery sack from behind her back. "I, um, bought a couple of things. The nurse told me it was his birthday."

"Oh, Mom." Lara pressed her lips together. "It's great. Come on in."

"Is he hurt?" Ava sat on the tiniest edge of the bed, almost like she felt like she didn't deserve to be there. Had Lara made her feel like that?

"He's doing great. He had a little cut on his forehead where something flew around in the car. A few bruises from the car-seat straps. Other than that, he's totally fine." She played with the strap on the bag. "I guess you think it's weird that I stayed here with him. And you're right, I probably should've dropped him off, but they're still looking for his family."

Ava's eyes were huge in her thin face. "I understand why you wanted to be with him. You were on your own so much as a child. You want to keep him from being alone."

"Yeah," Lara whispered. "I don't want him to be alone."

Ava looked away, dug into the bag. "So let's see. We've got blue iced cupcakes with sprinkles. I bought candles and matches, too. I know it's probably against the rules—"

"But we won't tell." Lara laughed. "Now we just need some balloons. I should get Loreen to blow up some more of the gloves."

"Oh, wait here." Ava jumped to her feet. In a moment, she returned with a big mylar balloon with the number two on it.

Lara's heart melted. But it wasn't the balloon. It was the enormous smile on her mom's face. It lit up the room.

"Mom, it's perfect." Tears clogged her throat and were making her nose run, but she refused to cry.

Ava giggled. "Okay, let's get started." She pulled a rolling tray over to the bed and set out six cupcakes, putting two candles in the one with the most icing.

Napkins followed the cupcakes out of the bag.

Brody looked at the table with wide baby-blue eyes. "Cake?" He smiled and pointed. "B'oon?"

Lara pulled the balloon where he could reach it. "Yep, it's a balloon and it's yours, big guy."

She reached for her mom's hand. "This is the happiest he's been since we brought him in. You did this."

Ava's bottom lip trembled, but she firmed it. "It's really not very much, considering he doesn't have his mom."

Lara stopped pulling things out of the bag and turned to her mother. "Mom—"

"Hey, is this a closed party?" Matt stood in the doorway. "I heard you were still here and thought I'd see if you needed a ride back to the station."

Matt was in his uniform—his blue work pants and SBFD T-shirt only accentuating his dark good looks. His nearly black hair curling over his forehead made Lara's fingers itch to brush it back.

"Come on in. I don't think you met Brody at the accident."

"I didn't. Hey, buddy-boy, how old are you?"

Brody's face scrunched up and he looked down at his fingers.

Matt helped him make a peace sign with his two fingers. "There you go. Two years old."

"Two!" Brody yelled.

Lara lit the candles on Brody's birthday cupcake. Matt started the "Happy Birthday" song and as they finished and clapped, Lara held the cupcake out for Brody. "Blow out the candles, little man. Ready, one-two-three!"

She helped him blow out the two tiny birthday candles. He smiled, a big baby-toothed grin, and clapped.

The nurses stopped by to wish Brody a happy birthday, too. As they went back to their patients, Ava handed them a cupcake, leaving just enough for Brody and Matt and one for her and Lara to share. Lara let Brody stick his fingers in the cake.

He stuck his fingers in his mouth, grabbed his cup off the table and flopped back on his pillow. He stared at the balloon floating above him and pointed with blue sticky fingers, taking them out of his mouth long enough to say, "B'oon."

Ava cleaned up what little mess there was, mostly crumbs from Brody's cupcake. Lara rubbed his hair gently, and his eyes drifted closed.

"What'll happen to him now?" Ava whispered, but her voice hitched. "Poor little man."

"Well, they're looking for any family that he might have, but unless they find someone tonight, he'll probably go into foster care, at least for a while." She brushed his bangs out of his face and pulled the sheet up to cover him.

"Poor little guy." Matt pulled a toy car out of his pocket and laid it on the table beside the bed.

"Where'd you get that?" Lara touched it and it rolled across the tray.

"I have my sources." He rolled his eyes. "Gift shop?"

Ava picked up the bag of stuff and held it in front of her. "Thanks, Lara."

"For what? Mom, you brought the party. It was an amazing thing for you to do." And it was. It was also a humbling experience for Lara, to realize that there was more to her mom than their past and her own pain.

"That mother who was drunk and had a wreck. It could've been me. That's why you feel for this baby so much, isn't it? It reminds you of me." Her mom perched on the edge of the visitor's chair, twisting the zipper pull on her jacket.

"A little, yeah." Brody was asleep, so Lara eased onto the bottom of the bed to sit. Exhaustion stalked her, something she hadn't noticed until now. She rubbed a hand over her forehead. "I saw the birthday stuff smashed all over their car and I remembered what it was like to have a mother who drank. Who didn't remember birthdays or worse, who did and ruined them by being drunk."

Matt shifted in the chair. "Um, maybe I should go."

Ava didn't move, just sat looking at the tiny kid in the bed, the one who had reminded Lara of herself.

Guilt sat like a knot in Lara's stomach. "I'm sorry, Mom. I'm tired and not really able to censor myself. We should both probably go get some rest."

"No." Ava said it firmly. "You deserve to say whatever you want to me. Your childhood was a nightmare and it was my fault."

Out of the corner of her eye, Lara saw Matt look longingly at the door.

"It was the disease, Mom." Lara answered

her quietly but as firmly as her mother had answered her. "You have a disease."

Lara slid off the bed, walked over to her mom and as she stood in front of her, recognized the beauty there, maybe for the first time. Despite understanding how hard her mom had been working this year to turn her life around, to stay stable, Lara hadn't stopped to tell Ava how proud she was of her.

She crouched in front of her mom, resting her hands on her knees. "Yes, I wish my childhood had been different. But, Mom, I love you."

Tears were running down her mother's face. "I'm so sorry, baby. I'm so sorry."

It wasn't the first time her mother had apologized. Over the years it had become a common refrain. Sorry she'd used the money Lara had for groceries on her drinking habit. Sorry she hadn't made it home last night. Sorry she forgot Lara's school play/birthday/softball game.

Maybe this time she meant it. Regardless, this time Lara accepted it. "I'm sorry, too. And I'm so proud of you for taking your meds, for doing the right thing. I know it's a struggle every day."

She'd learned from Matt as he talked to Emmy that love didn't come from her. It came from God. And God had enough love for both her and her mom.

Ava wrapped her arms around Lara. And as she sat there in her mother's arms for the first time she could ever remember, she realized things were changing faster than she could keep up. Maybe her mom's good mental health would last. Lara prayed that it would.

More than anything she wanted to be able to accept her the way she was right this minute and not always be thinking about tomorrow.

The nurse peeked her head around the corner. "Hey, I have good news. We found Brody's dad. He should be here within the hour to pick him up."

Some changes were good.

Some not so good.

Matt stood and stretched. "Why don't I take your mom to the hotel so she can get some rest, and then I'll come back for you? Brody's dad should be here by that time."

Lara sent him a grateful look, this man who by his presence alone made her feel cared for. "You know, I think that would be a great idea."

She and her mom would be checking into a hotel tonight instead of going home because her home, her every space, had been invaded by strangers who wished to do her harm. And no matter how serene these moments with Brody had been, danger seemed to lurk around every corner.

THIRTEEN

Matt walked into the kitchen at the station to find Johnny and True, from B Shift, eating Lara's stew. "Where's Lara?"

She'd called from her cell phone to let him know she'd caught a ride to the station with the ambulance crew who'd had a medical run.

True scooped another bite of stew into his mouth and talked around it. "She came in a little while ago, dished up the stew and left. You just missed her by a coupla seconds."

"Did you have some of this?" Johnny shoveled in a bite and chewed, literally groaning with pleasure. "I've eaten two bowls already. It's delicious."

Johnny hefted another huge spoonful.

Matt shoved True's face toward his plate of stew. "Thanks for the help."

He slung the strap of his bag over his shoulder

and headed out the door, calling out to whoever might be listening. "Later."

Rounding the corner for the parking lot, he dug in his pocket for the keys. "Come on, seriously?"

Not finding them in any of his pockets, he stuffed his hand down into the bottom of his bag. Finally, in desperation he shook his bag and heard them jingle at the bottom. He unzipped the pocket on the side of his bag and found them.

Out of the corner of his eye, he caught movement at the far end of the parking lot, a struggle.

Lara.

He dropped his bag and keys and sprinted for her. The man was straddling her, holding her down, face pushed into the gravel parking lot.

In the late-afternoon sunlight, Matt saw something gleam in the man's hand. A syringe.

"Stop! Lara!" Matt, used to dealing with split-second decisions, made one. He stomped on the attacker's ankle.

Her assailant roared and swiveled around to face Matt. In that tiny window of inattention, Lara got her wrist free and punched her attacker in the face. He reeled back.

As Matt circled, the man scrambled back,

his eyes burning dark in the holes of the mask. Matt lifted one booted foot and kicked him off Lara.

The syringe went flying.

The man scrambled to his feet and ran. He paused only to pick up the syringe before jumping into a paneled van parked on the other side of the parking lot. Tires squealed as he rounded the corner too fast. Matt tore after it, trying to get a look at the license plate, but it was obscured by mud. Perfect.

He ran back to Lara, who was tentatively testing her arms and legs. "You okay?"

"Yes. Fine. Just really ticked off. It takes some nerve to try something in the parking lot at the station." She pushed to her feet, brushing dirt and tiny rocks from her pant legs. "Ow."

Matt grabbed her hands and turned them up. Tiny cuts covered her palms. A whirlwind of worry and anger—mostly anger—built inside him. "Come on, let's go."

"My car is right here."

He dropped his hands. "Please?"

She didn't argue, just followed him to his car. "Mom's settled at the hotel, so she's fine, but I need to call her and let her know I'll be late."

Wordlessly he pulled his cell phone from his pocket and handed it to her. The blind rage that someone would attack her and that he'd almost been too late to stop it—that was what was really sticking in his craw. He'd been too late to stop her from being hurt.

He opened the door for her on the passenger side of his car. She shot him a puzzled look, but slid into the seat of his Charger.

Matt didn't say a word during the ride to his house. He couldn't, didn't dare, for fear he would say something that would scare her off. She'd only just begun to trust him on a personal level. And now this.

It killed him.

At his front door, he opened it for her, letting her go in first and taking a second to waggle his fingers at the little girls from next door, whose faces were glued to the side windows of their door.

"Go sit in the kitchen and I'll get the first-aid kit." He stalked into the hall bathroom and dug through the closet for the kit.

When he came back, she hadn't moved from the spot. "Why are you still there?"

"I'm just not used to seeing you act like this."

"Like what?"

She gave him the evaluating look she usually reserved for patients. "Like I'm a girl."

"You *are* a girl, if you haven't noticed." He turned the first-aid kit in his hands.

"Yeah, but I'm a girl that can haul a two-hundred-twenty-pound man out of a burning building. What gives?" She laughed and walked toward him.

His skin prickled. He turned away. She was getting a little too close. "Maybe I think of you like a sister."

"In that case, you'd be pulling my hair and kicking the backs of my heels when I walk." Her tone was gently teasing.

Reaching around, he snagged her ponytail, giving it a slight tug. "Better?"

When she laughed, he said, "Come on."

He opened the back door and flipped a light switch. Above them on the deck, twinkle lights draped from the four posts flickered to life. Another flip of a switch and lanterns hung from the branches of the trees in the yard became two-dozen tiny fireflies.

He sat down beside her and opened the first-aid kit. "I need to clean your hands."

Obediently, she held them out palms up. He poured hydrogen peroxide over them and, with gauze, cleaned the dirt and gravel.

Water lapped against the sea wall, the sound soothing after a ragged-edged day.

"I love it here." Lara leaned back against the cushion as he dabbed antibiotic ointment on the deepest cuts. "What made you buy it?"

"I wanted to live on the water, but beachfront property is out of my league. When I found this place on the canal it was a total dump. I renovated Alisha's side first, rented it to her and used the rent money to fix up my side." He placed a bandage—this one with multi-colored peace signs—over the deepest cut on the heel of her hand.

"How did you know?" Her voice was sleepy. "That you could make something beautiful out of it?"

A puff of a breeze, and with it came the scent of the jasmine blooming on the fence next door. "I knew this house had good bones and if I was willing to do the hard work it would be worth it."

She was silent for a minute, the quiet slap of the water the only sound. "I think there's a lot more to you than your dad sees."

His heartbeat seemed to stop for a moment then kicked back into gear with a stutter and a skip. "What—what makes you think my dad has any issue with me?"

"I heard the way he talked the other night about your being a firefighter. It was subtle but it was there." She raised a hand. "Hel-*lo,* raised in dysfunction here. I have a little experience. But he's wrong. You're a natural leader, even more so because it's not something you put on—it's just who you are."

"Hmm." Matt shifted on the seat, not sure he was entirely comfortable with being analyzed.

She smiled. "It took me a while to figure out. Especially since you were always baby powdering someone's bunk."

"Or putting it up on soda cans?"

"Oh, yeah, how could I forget? That was *my* bed that came crashing to the floor when I got into it."

A laugh rumbled to the surface. "Yeah. That was a good one."

"It was the first time I'd ever felt a part, a real part, of anything." She turned her gaze over the black water of the canal.

I love you. The words came to his lips as naturally as breathing. He wanted to tell her, but the trust between them was a fragile link, a tentative wire that could be broken so easily. So instead of saying the words, he put his arm around her and pulled her close, snug against his body.

And in his world, the pieces clicked into

place. He raised his head and looked at her, wondering if she heard them, too.

She relaxed against him, her eyes closed, toe barely touching the deck, just enough to keep them moving. Her hair, silk against his shoulder, gleamed in the glow of the twinkle lights.

And his phone buzzed in his pocket. He wanted to throw it into the canal.

She stirred. "Don't you need to get that?"

"Yes." He didn't move, just pushed the swing to make it rock a few more times.

She chuckled against his chest.

He blew out a frustrated breath but reached for the phone. It caught on his pocket, but he managed to pull it out and check the readout without completely dislodging Lara.

Without a doubt, though, their quiet interlude was over. Tyler had news and would be at his house in ten.

"My brother Tyler's on his way here. He'll be here in ten minutes." Matt shoved the phone back in his pocket.

"Wait. *Tyler?*"

"And I think it's time we bring Cruse Conyers in, too. This has gone on long enough. If we're going to take these dealers and manu-facturers down, it's going to take all of us work-ing together." Was he purposely ignoring her or just doing that typical convenient lack-of-hearing thing that guys did?

"So do you want to tell me what's going on with your brother?" She really wasn't nosy and certainly she understood better than anyone about keeping your family business in the family, but this was important.

"Tyler showed up at my house last night. He's the inside informant."

Wow. Lara reeled at the new info. "How does he know about these men?"

"According to him, he's living with them. Undercover in the Diablo Brotherhood. He has been for eighteen months." Matt picked up the first-aid stuff and packed it in the kit.

"More than a year? Wow. Do you believe him?"

He stopped on the way to the kitchen but didn't turn around. "He's my brother, Lara."

"You know your mom thinks he's just out there somewhere."

He sighed, a huge indrawing of breath and release. "Knowing this would be way worse. She told you about Ethan's family?"

When she nodded, he went on. "Ethan was working for the FBI. He'd been undercover for seven months and was within hours of closing his case. His wife and baby boy were killed because the criminals he was working with found out he was a cop. I guess they figured it would be worse punishment to kill his family than to kill him. They were right."

"Oh, Matt." She walked toward him and reached for his hand, the salve on hers making them sticky.

"We can use the information Tyler gives us, but unless he offers, I'm not going to say where I got it. It puts him in too much danger. I'm not sure my mother would survive another blow like the one she took when Ethan's family died." Matt squeezed her hand, tugged her closer.

Her entire body three or four inches away from his, she looked up into his dark brown eyes. "So what, really, do we know?"

"Not enough. Emmy told me today that she bought drugs at The Sand Dollar Club and picked up packages to run to J. So we need to fill Cruse in."

"The Sand Dollar on Sea Breeze Beach?"

"Yes, it's right here on our home grounds. So we'll let Cruse figure out the next move, let him fight it out with the Feds. But regardless, it's time to put this case away before anyone else we care about gets hurt."

"I agree. I'll go make some coffee while you get Cruse on the phone."

"Good idea." As she started to reach for the doorknob, he pulled her in for a quick, hard kiss.

Her eyes widened in surprise. "Just for making coffee?"

He grinned. "Never underestimate the power."

"Yeah, yeah. Get busy. We have work to do."

As she opened the back door, she laughed again, a sweet, happy sound, and he couldn't help but wonder.

With so much at stake, could it possibly last?

Lara spooned Lucky Charms into her mouth while Matt prowled his kitchen, opening and closing glossy cherry cabinet doors.

"I didn't get anything to eat. Those yahoos on B shift ate all the stew. And I don't even have a can of tomato soup." He slammed the cabinet door and picked up the coffeepot, sloshing coffee onto the counter.

"Lucky Charms are pretty good," Lara said around a mouthful of sweet, sticky marshmallows and crunchy bits of cereal.

"Those are for the kids next door. I do have Raisin Bran."

"Ew, no. That would be healthy."

"Oh, right. And we wouldn't want that. You do know you have a problem, right? First step is admitting it." Matt was trying so hard to be normal. They both knew this situation was anything but. Tension spiraled as they waited for the others. She could see it in Matt's posture, in his face.

"Matt, we're going to figure this out. You can relax." She put the spoon down on the table and reached out to grab his hand. "Really. Please relax."

"It's not that." He stopped, facing the sink, his hands stretched out to grip the edge of his honed granite countertop, his head down. "They tried to kidnap you today. If I hadn't— Lara, if I hadn't come around the corner, they might have succeeded."

It was her. He was upset about her, not the case. "But they didn't. I'm fine. I'm right here."

"The guy had a needle ready to stick in your arm." He turned to face her, his eyes miserable. "Every time I think about it—"

She laid her spoon down on the table. "It didn't happen. You stopped it. What's the deal, Matt? You've saved my behind multiple times in fire situations."

"I have no idea. You'd think I'd be used to you getting yourself in dangerous situations."

"You're such a man." She picked her bowl up from the table and walked it back to the sink, dumping it and filling it with water again.

He laughed. "Yeah, and?"

Someone tapped on the back door. Lara jumped.

Flipping the light off in the kitchen, he opened the door to let in Tyler Clark. She'd never met him before, only seen his picture. He looked like Matt, but harder. Taller, leaner, deeper lines in his face.

"Conyers is behind me."

Cruse Conyers slid in the back door and closed it behind him. "I asked Chloe Rollins to come since she's been in on this from the beginning. She should be here in a few minutes. It takes some time to make sure there's no one following."

Tyler sprawled in one of the kitchen chairs. "As far as I could tell, no one is watching. They were scared this afternoon after they went for you and missed."

He was talking to Lara, but he barely looked at her. It was like he couldn't rejoin the real world until he was no longer a part of that undercover world he was living in.

Cruse pulled some papers out of his back pocket. "I got some info on that name you gave me. Alfred Baxter. He's young. Twenty-two. Chemistry major from Tulane University. I had Maria run down one of his professors. Supposedly, he's brilliant. He never finished his degree, though."

"Because he's busy here cooking up illegal drugs." Matt shook his head as the doorbell rang.

Chloe walked in and handed Lara a plate with a couple of dozen cookies on it. "I figured plain sight was better—I'm just a friend bringing some food to a couple of pals who've had a bad day."

"Good idea—and thanks. The others are in the kitchen."

Matt's arm snaked around her to grab a cookie.

She pulled them away. "Hey!"

"You're not the only one who had a bad day. I deserve a cookie." He stuffed it in his mouth and groaned, rolling his eyes to look at Chloe. "Homemade?"

"Don't look at me. Jake makes cookies when he gets stressed. I go to the range and shoot things." Chloe walked toward the kitchen, her silky red ponytail swinging.

Around Matt's table in the dark kitchen, Tyler filled them in. "The supply of Bright Orange is almost depleted, so the Brotherhood have found a new house to use as a lab. They haven't told me where it is yet, but I think I can find out."

Police Captain Conyers narrowed his eyes in thought. "I know we've got these guys cold with Tyler's testimony and Emmy's, but this job, this setup seems a little too complicated even for the Diablo Brotherhood. They seem more like enforcers than the brains behind the effort."

Chloe took a cookie from the plate on the table and picked at it.

Matt turned to Tyler. "Is that true? Are they just the enforcers?"

Tyler nodded slowly. "Yes and no. They've got some power here because they know the product and what it takes to manufacture it. They own the circulation because they've put the lean on local drug dealers to open their lines of distribution."

"Like Baby J." It wasn't a question from Matt but a statement of fact.

Tyler looked at him, surprised. "Yeah, like Baby J. But I don't know this Baxter guy. He came into the picture before I did. He 'recruited' Emmy?"

Matt nodded. "I think he was looking for a

mule, someone who wouldn't be suspicious. He hit on the idea of using a former junkie. Pretty, needy, she fits in with a certain crowd. And if she gets caught with the drugs, it's all on her."

"So my question is—who recruited him?" Cruse looked around the table from one serious face to the other.

Lara didn't want to take part in this conversation, felt way out of her league. But… "I think maybe the center of the operation is this club that Emmy went to when she wanted to buy the drug."

"They definitely meet there, but I've never been in on the meetings." Tyler crossed his arms, impatience and annoyance grooved into the lines of his face. "We don't have time for a court order and surveillance and all that. This thing is about to explode."

"There's one thing." Every head swiveled to look at Lara.

"Emmy's been there. She's a drug addict. It's not like someone would be surprised if she left rehab and came back. She and I look just alike."

Matt didn't hesitate. "No."

Cruse Conyers and Tyler Clark looked at each other across the table. She could tell they were thinking about it.

Cruse tapped his finger on the table. "Chloe has undercover experience. She could go in with her."

Tyler steepled his fingers and pointed them at Cruse. "I could try to convince them that they need a meeting with the boss, make sure everyone's on the same page. I didn't grow up with them, so they don't exactly trust me, but they do listen to me."

"No." Matt said it again, more forcefully.

Lara understood his response. She was his partner. He was conditioned to protect her. And considering the conversation they'd just had it made even more sense, but she had to act. She couldn't sit by and do nothing and watch other people suffer like Emmy did.

She looked around the table. "Could you guys give us a minute?"

Cruse and Chloe slid their chairs back from the table and went into the front room. Tyler was slower to move.

He looked at his little brother. "Don't ruin our best chance of getting the proof we need to take these people down, Matt. They wouldn't hesitate to do the same to you."

Tyler turned and left the room. Matt stood to pace, pent-up feelings on his face and in the taut lines of his body. At the end of the small room, he wheeled to face her. "I know they wouldn't hesitate to take us down. They've tried. More than once. If they even suspect that you're not Emmy, it's over."

"Then I'll have to be better than they are. I can do this, Matt. I *need* to do this. My whole life I've tried to change things. I tried to change things for my mom. You know how that turned out. I tried to change things for Emmy. Again, great results there."

Matt's mouth set in a hard line as he leaned against his refrigerator and crossed his arms. "I think you're underestimating what you do for them."

"I have the power to really change things for a lot of people. How could I live with myself if I didn't do it?"

She pushed away from the table and walked to face him, rubbed his arms gently until he relented. She didn't know what her feelings were for this complicated man, but she did know that they were deep and confusing. She needed time, after this was all over, to figure things out.

Finally, he reached for her, pulling her close. "I can't stand this."

Lara closed her eyes, breathed in Matt's scent, spicy and familiar, uniquely him. And just there, it all seemed to make sense. She sighed. "I won't be able to do this without you."

His arms tightened around her. "I'll be right outside every step of the way."

A throat cleared at the door. Lara jerked, but Matt didn't release her, just tightened his arms even more. "Don't let anything happen to her, Cruse."

"We'll plan it the best way we know how, which is going to take time." Cruse turned and called the others into the room.

Lara stepped out of Matt's arms and immediately felt the loss. But she knew that she had to get used to it. She would be trying to fool some very dangerous people into believing that she was her sister. Trying to fool them into giving something away. Something that would put them in prison.

She could only hope that she was strong enough to pull it off.

FOURTEEN

Matt sat in a surveillance van outside The Sand Dollar Club. It was a rattletrap shack of a beach club, the wood siding having long given up the battle against the elements, but it was situated at the end of a pier stretching into the bay. A fantastic view of the sunset made it a popular watering hole both for locals and tourists alike despite its weathered appearance.

He wasn't as close as he'd like to be, but their equipment would hold. Probably. They had visual and audio in the club. At the very last minute, a federal judge had come through with a court order for the surveillance. A string of cops and federal agents had been going in surreptitiously, hanging out for a while and placing the bugs and tiny cameras.

Even those had their limitations, but according to the blueprints the city had, the club had several smaller rooms hooked together, with a very small one-room office upstairs. The product of expanding over many years.

They'd be putting a wire on Lara. Chloe would be wired, too, and she would be in the building with Lara, eyes on. The plan, for short notice, was as clean as they could make it. He didn't want her to take the risk—even though he was so proud of her that she would. It would be so much easier to deal with it if he were the one facing the danger.

In the quiet of the truck, Matt bowed his head. "Lord, I know You hear me. You care what happens in this community. And I know You care about Lara even more than I do. God, I pray You would keep her safe."

The door opened and Cruse Conyers stepped inside, followed by Maria Fuentes. The fiery forensics specialist was better at running the technology than the tech guys. And she would recognize evidence when she saw it.

She immediately sat at the main console and started typing, clarifying the images, setting the digital recorders.

Cruse picked his way through the maze of wires until he could sit. Deliberately, he placed a key card on the console beside Matt. "Chloe just went in. You probably have about ten minutes if you want to see Lara before she goes in. She's in unit 108 in that condo to our left."

Matt sat without moving, thoughts circling in his mind. Would that really be a good idea? He hadn't seen her since he'd said goodbye to her in front of Cruse and Tyler the other night. She'd been closeted in the condo with Chloe, taking a crash course in going undercover.

With a jerk of his head, Cruse flipped his surfer blond hair out of his eyes. "Don't tell me you're going to let the woman you love go into that club without telling her."

"What—" Matt began.

Cruse interrupted him. "Oh, come on. Do you think I don't recognize that look on your face? I've seen it in the mirror. I know it's scarier than facing the worst fire you've ever seen. I've been there. Maria—well, Maria hasn't, but she's too cranky for a boyfriend."

A spare headset hit Cruse in the forehead. "Ouch! I was kidding, Maria. But it seems to me that kind of proved my point."

"Cranky shmanky. If you had to work with all this testosterone day after day, you'd be cranky, too. Matt, what Cruse is trying to say is tell the woman you love her. You may not get another chance." Her fingers never paused in their typing.

"Thanks, Maria. As if I wasn't worried enough." He took his headset off and laid it on the console, snagging the key card from the desk beside him. "But your point is taken."

"Good. You can bring me some more coffee when you come back." She tapped her pencil on the readout, hmmed for a second and went back to typing.

Matt opened the door and walked the couple of hundred feet to the condo, his heart pounding worse than it ever had when he was going into a fire. This time he was going in with no backup.

He stood outside the first-floor condominium, trying to breathe. He gave himself a few seconds to collect his thoughts, slid the key card into the lock and opened the door.

She wasn't there.

Looking around the room, Matt saw signs that she and Chloe and Maria had dressed in the room. Scattered bits of tape and makeup dusted the surfaces.

The two women had been staying here the last couple of days. An open box of Cookie Crisp lay on its side on the counter, cereal spilling out, the prize packet torn open. He picked up the prize, turned it in his hands—a carry-along container, so you were never without a supply of your favorite cereal, he guessed.

Just as he was about to turn around to leave, he heard the bathroom door open.

He stood there, stunned. Lara looked exactly like Emmy. Clothes swallowed what looked like an emaciated body. Her hair hung in limp ropes across her shoulders. Eyes were sunken and ringed with deep circles and heavy makeup. Her complexion was sallow and her lips ringed with sores.

"I know, right?" She plucked at her short denim skirt. "Maria wired me up and Chloe did the makeup job. Apparently she has some experience impersonating a drug addict."

Matt took a deep breath. Now or never. He waded in, not giving himself the chance to back out. "Lara, I love you."

He stopped her as her mouth fell open to argue. "You don't have to say anything—it's just important that you know how I feel about you. And I *love* you."

Saying the words again, he realized that he'd never meant them more in his life. His nervousness disappeared like smoke in the wind. He loved her and that's all that mattered.

She shook her head slowly. "For a little while yesterday, on your back porch, being with you felt like magic. And I thought maybe… But Matt, look at me. This costume *is* me. This is my life and it always has been, starting with my mom and now Emmy. My life is a mess."

And there was the rub. She honestly believed that. Honestly believed that she was unlovable, or somehow not worthy of his love. Maybe she thought, despite everything they'd been through, he still didn't know her enough to really love her.

He took a step closer. "I love that when we work together you don't push in front of me. You don't follow behind me, but on every fire, we go through the door together, side by side. I love your sense of humor. I love your courage. I love that you are stubborn enough to fight for your position even when you know you're wrong."

One tear began a slow track down her cheek. "Matt—"

He forged on. "I love that you drink your Diet Coke at the same exact time every day. That you eat kids' cereal for breakfast, lunch and dinner. I love that you wear your hair in a ponytail at work but take it down as soon as your feet hit the parking lot. I love your heart—that you would put your family ahead of yourself."

She was fighting full-out tears, blinking them

back. She stomped one combat-booted foot. "I cannot mess this makeup up."

He laughed and wrapped his arms around her, placing a kiss at her hairline. And in his arms, he could feel his sturdy partner. "Most of all, babe, I love that when I'm with you, you make me want to fight for a better world."

She pulled back to look at him, and in her eyes he could see the regret. His heart squeezed.

"Matt, this getup—" she waved a hand at her clothes. "—this outer shell may not be who you see, but it is who I see."

She walked to the counter and picked up the toy that he'd just been holding. "Do you know why I have a thing for kids' cereal?"

He met her at the counter.

"When we were kids, we couldn't afford cereal. I saw the boxes in the store. They looked so good, so bright and yummy. And they had prizes in them. But we were hungry, and I could barely scrape together enough change to buy a loaf of bread and a jar of peanut butter so Emmy and I wouldn't starve." She righted the box on the counter and very carefully closed the flaps. "I promised myself that one day I would buy whatever I wanted at the grocery store."

His throat stung, the magnitude of what she'd overcome only making him respect her more.

"Don't you see, Matt? It's only by the grace of God that I'm not Emmy. I so easily could be."

He wanted to pull her close again, wanted to wrap her in his safe embrace and never let her go. Instead he had to remain cool. Forcing the issue would only push her away. "You're right, Lara, but you're also wrong. It's only by the grace of God that any of us succeed. There are so many ways we can mess it up. But that's what makes life beautiful, you know? When you recognize what a gift it is and choose to live to honor it."

Her eyes narrowed in thought, but he could still see the doubt. Her lips parted and in his earpiece he heard Cruse Conyers's voice. "Chloe just gave the signal. Lara, you ready?"

Matt had forgotten all about the fact that she wore a mic. Great. Everyone on this op had heard him bare his soul.

He didn't care. He loved her. If he made a fool out of himself to prove it, so be it.

She took a step away but still held eye contact, her hazel eyes wide, pupils dilating as her heart rate increased. "I'm ready, Cruse. I'll be at the door to the club in three minutes."

Lara turned and walked through the door, never looking back.

Matt closed his eyes, lifting a silent prayer to

God for her safety. Really silent. He didn't even know the words to use for how full his heart was of her.

For her.

But God knew. And Matt prayed that the team of people watching out for her would be enough.

Jimmy Buffett blared as Lara pushed open the door of the beachfront club. A dingy wooden building, the salty sea air had been rough on it. She had to focus on acting jittery. Not that it was very hard. She was about to jump out of her skin.

A large wooden bar stretched across one side of the room. The patrons were a mix of locals and summer visitors. They weren't usually dressed too differently, but the tourists were almost always sunburned. There were a couple of scary-looking customers in the back of the room whom she kind of let her eyes skim over. They were certainly keeping their eyes on her.

She'd acted tough, but she was scared out of her mind. There were so many places this plan could go wrong. But, like the others, she knew that Tyler had manufactured their one chance to figure out who was actually the driving force behind the development of the superlabs and Bright Orange.

Lara wove her way through the patrons and perched on a stool at one of the few empty tables. The waitress came by with a tray full of empties. Lara grabbed her sleeve and ordered a drink—it was what Emmy would've done. Her eyes glided around the club again, barely hesitating as she caught Chloe's eye, instead lighting on the poster of the Navy's Blue Angels above her head.

The door of the club slammed open and Tyler Clark strode in. Instead of his black baggy jeans and hoodie, he wore black pants and a T-shirt. His nearly black hair was slicked up in the front. Instead of the intense, highly intelligent agent she'd met, here was a surly, dangerous hoodlum. When he leaned on the bar, the bartender didn't dally but served him immediately.

Two men pushed away from a table and joined Tyler at the bar. Both had the same dragon tattoo that Tyler had on his left biceps. One of the men had his head nearly shaved and sported earrings in both ears. The other pointed at Lara. Tyler stared at her, his eyes narrowed in menace. He nodded, still maintaining that threatening stare and patted his waist, like he was showing them that he was carrying a gun.

He sauntered over to her. She backed away. The fear wasn't really an act. He looked like he would shoot her as soon as look at her.

Tyler leaned on the scarred wooden table took a slug from the drink she wasn't drinking. "That didn't take long. They noticed you as soon as you came in the door. The boss isn't here yet and they can't decide whether to deal with you themselves or give him the pleasure."

She swallowed hard, backed up a little, her shoulders jerking. "I just want the stuff."

"Yeah, I know, Emmy." Tyler leaned forward, the threat on his face. His voice was low. She had to strain to hear it over the music. "I'll try to get them to take you upstairs so they won't disturb the crowd down here. Chances are just as good that they'll try to drag you out the door, so you should be ready. You've got backup, so don't worry."

He picked her drink up and drained it. "See ya."

She watched him saunter back to his group. He was almost too real. Was there ever a point, she wondered, when the line blurred so much that he didn't know where it was?

She wished she had her partner sitting beside her. She'd never felt vulnerable, not once, when she'd blown through a door with him by her side.

The door opened and this time it was four tourists, their skin glowing red from too much time spent in the sun. Before the door could even close again, someone limped in. The face was partially covered with a hat, but when Lara looked closer, she realized it was Baby J.

His bodyguard pushed him and he lurched forward, his hat flying off. Her stomach churned. His eyes were swollen almost shut, his face so bruised she could hardly see any normal-colored skin. She breathed the question. "Why?"

In her tiny earpiece, Cruse answered. "It would've been pretty obvious who told where your sister was. And then once we pulled him in, he was history. The only reason they didn't kill him is that they need him."

Lara scratched her nose so no one would see her lips move. "Why would he risk it?"

This time it was Maria's voice. "Because Matt saved his brother three years ago. The medics got to the scene first. They're supposed to wait for the cops when there are shots fired, and in this case there were still shots being fired. Baby J's kid brother had been hit. He was dying."

"I patched him up, end of story. J feels like he owes me." Matt's voice was firm, annoyed.

Maria cut in. "Not quite. No one would help—it was too dangerous. But Matt could see the kid had a pneumothorax. He was struggling to breathe. Matt ran for them, taking a bullet in the process."

"Oh." Lara breathed the reply. It was just like Matt, his heart so full of compassion for the hurting that he would risk his own life to help someone he saw in need.

Matt again. "You know, that bodyguard isn't a very good bodyguard. He doesn't have a scratch on him. Something tells me…"

Chloe finished his sentence from the other side of the room from Lara. "He isn't really a bodyguard. He's one of the Brotherhood. Check out the tattoo."

Cruse Conyers put the pieces together. "So he was put there to keep Baby J in line. I think we've got the Diablo Brotherhood as the manufacturing and enforcing end. Baby J is the distributor to the public. We still need to know who developed the drug. Who's in charge."

One of the men standing with Tyler Clark pulled a cell phone out of his pocket. His eyes searched the club and landed on Lara. He nodded his head, spoke into the phone and closed it. Taking one step forward, he motioned to the other men.

"Let's go." She could read his lips clearly. Her insides quaked. This is what she wanted to happen. She needed to get to the office upstairs to find out who would bring this horrible drug into their community. Who would be cruel enough to specifically target recovering addicts like her sister.

The entire menacing group, five of them, started toward her. As they got closer, the bodyguard pushed Baby J onto the table. His eyes were watery slits, but he peered up at her. "I gave you a chance. You should've stayed away."

She shrugged and looked away, sliding the strap of her tank top back to her shoulder.

One of the men grabbed her by the arm, digging thick fingers into the muscle. "Come on, let's go."

"Where are we going? Look, dude, all I want is a hit. Please, just give it to me. I've got money." She pulled a wad of cash out of her pocket.

He dragged her toward the stairs, the other men flanking the rear, with Baby J between them. She managed to catch Chloe's eye as they pulled her past the bar.   •

She wasn't worried that they would find the wire. Maria was a genius and had hidden it so well that no one, short of taking apart her clothes at the seams, would ever guess she was wearing it.

"Stop. I'll do whatever you want. Just give me the drugs." Lara made her voice sound high and strung out. It wasn't very hard with the adrenaline flooding her veins.

"Shut up." The man they'd thought was Baby J's bodyguard shoved her against the wall. "You only get drugs when you do what we want. Remember how that works?"

Just as she wanted to punch the guy in the face, she heard Chloe's voice in her ear. "Remember you have to respond like Emmy would. You're doing great, girl. You can do this."

Lara slumped like she'd seen Emmy do countless times, flicking him away with a fluttery hand. "I'll do whatever you say. Just get me what I need."

He pulled her close, his breath hot on her ear. "Now that's more like it. I like a cooperative chick." He pulled the cash out of her hand and stuffed it into his own pocket.

She closed her eyes. She could do this. As much as she hated the feeling this man gave her, she knew Emmy had hated it just as much but hadn't known a way out.

"Hey, babe. I know this is tough. Hang in there, okay?" Matt's voice in her ear. She didn't know whether to feel relieved or ashamed, but she had nothing to feel guilty or ashamed about. It was these men who were doing this. They had victimized her sister and would do their best to take advantage of her.

Her resolve firmed. She would be no man's victim, but if it took acting like one to send these criminals to prison, then that's exactly what she would do.

"Okay, okay. Let's go." She pushed past the man and looked up. There at the top of the stairs was her objective. The man behind this whole thing.

Matt peered at the screen, straining to hear every nuance in Lara's voice. "I don't see her."

Maria leaned back, which, in the van, put her head right by Matt's ear. "She's on audio but not video at this point, loverboy."

In his headset, he heard static and then a word, "…boss…door…*Burke?*"

He whipped around to Maria. "What did she say? What's wrong with it?"

Maria was tapping buttons. She didn't even turn around.

Matt looked at Cruse.

Cruse shook his head.

"…fix…money…"

"Did he say it?" Matt had his hands on his earphones staring into the screen, as if that would somehow magically make the transmission more clear. "How are we supposed to hear the go signal if it's breaking up?"

Chloe's voice burst through the connection, the clarity nearly earsplitting after straining to hear every word from Lara. "You don't want to do that."

Matt got even closer to the screen if that was even possible. "Wait. Does that look like—is that smoke?"

"Chloe, what's going on in there?" Cruse took a closer look at the monitor. "Not smoke, just interference or something."

Chloe's voice, strained nearly to the breaking point, came back over their connection. "Guys, we have a situation here."

"It is smoke." Matt whipped off the headphones. "Listen to me, Cruse. That building is tinder. It will go up in seconds. Lara is on the top floor and we need to get her out."

Vaguely, he registered Maria talking to the

emergency dispatcher requesting the fire department as he pushed past Cruse. Cruse grabbed his shirt. "You don't have the right equipment to go in. Think about this. All you're doing if you go is giving us someone else to rescue."

Matt snatched the headphones off the table. "Chloe, get out of there *now*. It's not safe." To Cruse he said, "I'm going in. I'm not leaving Lara in there to die."

Matt shoved open the door of the van and sprinted down the pier to the club, getting to the front door of the club as it slammed open and people poured out, staggering and coughing. One woman in spiked heels fell to the ground and nearly got trampled. Matt muscled his way into the crowd and helped her to her feet.

People were jumping off the pier into the water from the rear of the building, screaming. It went against everything he knew to leave them, but he knew his first priority had to be getting to Lara.

In his earpiece, he heard her voice, fading in and out. "Matt, if you're still listening—"

If he was listening. Dear Jesus, please, he just wanted to be face-to-face with her—*listening*.

Pushing through the stream of people, he bumped into Chloe. She held a bar towel over her face and her arm circled a young college student. "Get as far away from here as you can."

"Matt, I love you." His feet cemented to the pier as he focused on Lara's voice.

Chloe pulled the towel away from her face. Her words drifted back as the crowd carried her away. "Be careful in there. You can barely see."

He couldn't answer Lara. It was killing him. *Hang in there, baby. Hang on.*

"I can…smoke…under the door." Her connection was still fading in and out.

Galvanized by her words, Matt elbowed his way through the final push of people stampeding the door. Entering the building, he tried to take stock of his surroundings. He'd only seen the inside of the building from the video camera.

"I was afraid, Matt." *Was* afraid, not am afraid. He couldn't take this, hearing her soul-baring words and not being there.

"…thought you…never want me. You deserved so much more." She had no idea what she was worth. But he wanted to spend every day of the rest of his life showing her.

The room was wrapped in a shroud of curling, breathing smoke. Matt couldn't see where to go. He'd have to orient himself according to his memory of what the rooms looked like.

Tyler appeared like an apparition in the haze—his badge dangled around his neck on a chain and he dragged a man by handcuffs. Matt couldn't see the man's face—a T-shirt was wrapped around it.

"Where's Lara?"

Tyler's face was drawn in hard lines. "I don't know. A couple of the men pulled her out of the room I was in just as the fire started. I hope your boys were outside to catch the Diablos as they came out. They scattered like cockroaches." He coughed into his shoulder. "Matt, I'm sorry."

"Get out of here." Matt shoved past Tyler. The shirt fell away from the man's face. Under it, Matt saw the man who'd created the deadly drug, Alfred Baxter. Black hair and glasses—he looked exactly like the drawing that the police sketch artist had drawn.

Matt was past caring about the Diablo Brotherhood getting what they deserved. His first— his only—priority was finding Lara alive.

He heard her cough over the wire. And then by some miracle of sound waves, her words came through crystal clear. "I love you, Matt Clark, and I have from the beginning. You know me. You know it was…always easier for me to take the dare than to tell the truth."

His eyes stinging, he pulled the neck of his T-shirt up to cover his mouth and nose and dropped to his knees where the air was better. Upstairs first.

If he didn't find her up there, he could check the bottom floor, but if he waited, it would be too late. As hot as this fire was burning, the stairs would be gone. There'd be no way to get upstairs to search.

Hot orange flames licked the ceiling. The entire bar area was on fire. Point of origin. Alcohol and a lighter would do it and, depending on the mentality of the crowd, it would either be put out immediately or it would escalate into this.

At the base of the stairs, Matt looked up. Heat seared his skin from the fire in the room. Time was running out. On his hands and feet, he climbed the stairs, the palms of his hands burning. The office door stood open. He crab-walked the length of the small room.

Nothing. No closet to hide in. No one under the desk. He coughed, the heated air on the second floor scorching the tender skin of his throat. "Lara!"

Tyler had said they dragged her out. Was

it possible there was another room that they hadn't known about? On his hands and knees, he crawled out into the hall, coughed again. He couldn't see at all. His eyes streamed tears.

He swiped his arm across his eyes and dropped onto his chest. The floor was hot under his body. Not good. But from this position, he had an inch or two of better visibility and he could see the crack of a door to his right.

His soul reached heavenward. *Please, God.* He stretched up to touch the knob. No heat, but it was locked. Would they lock her in?

The answer to that question, an unequivocal yes. People who have so little a conscience as to manufacture drugs and sell them for profit wouldn't hesitate to kill someone they thought was going to get in their way.

What if they had killed her before the fire started?

He stood and kicked the door. It splintered, but the lock held. "Lara!"

Nothing. He couldn't hear anything. Thick smoke poured up the stairs, and a quick look at the flames licking up the wall told him that if he didn't get down those stairs fast, he'd be stranded.

Putting his shoulder to the door, he slammed

into it once, twice, and again. When the lock finally broke from the door, Matt pushed it open.

His father's friend, Owen Burke, stood behind rows of boxes at a wall safe, shoveling money into a duffel bag. "Uncle Owen?"

Owen's back stiffened. He reached into the safe one more time and turned around with a handgun. "Don't make this any harder than it already is, Matt."

"Why are you *doing* this?" Matt coughed, his eyes and nose running in the foul air.

"Oh, come on. Have you seen my businesses? Money has dried up. Restaurants and clubs that used to make money hand over fist are money pits. That kid Baxter was like a gift from the gods when I realized what I had." He zipped up the bag, leaving the safe hanging open, empty.

"Where's Lara?"

"Don't you mean Emmy?" Owen smiled and Matt could see that he had no remorse, no feeling at all.

"*Where is she,* Owen?"

Owen Burke edged toward the door, the gun still leveled at Matt. "Don't make me shoot you."

Matt let him go. They knew who it was. Owen would never get away clean.

And as he disappeared into the billowing smoke, Matt searched the room for Lara. She had to be here. He looked behind every row of boxes.

Hope vanished. He turned to leave.

But something told him not to leave without looking in every crevice and corner.

He dropped to his knees again, a spasm in his throat sending him into a coughing fit. If he didn't leave within seconds, he'd be caught in this building, too.

But behind the last row of boxes, he saw something weird. The smoke was being sucked under the wall. There was something—space—behind it.

He kicked at the wall with his foot. A piece gave way. He kicked it again. Tearing at it with his hands, he ripped pieces away until he had a hole big enough to see through.

Lara was on the floor, her hands and feet bound with duct tape.

Matt hacked the wallboard away, kicking and pulling until he could get to her. He lifted her into the larger room. Taking a knife from his pocket, he sliced through the tape and released her.

Her head lolled back, nostrils flaring as she

tried to get life-giving oxygen. Her hair was sweaty, her face ashy-gray from lack of air.

He had never wished for anything more than his SCBA equipment. He looked around the room. Nothing. In desperation, he fisted his hand and slammed it into the wall. He ripped a piece of wallboard away. Lifting her up, he quickly shoved her face into the space between the drywall and the outside wall.

He felt more than heard her take a deep breath. And another. She lifted her head.

Matt grinned. "Welcome back."

A sharp crack from the hall drew his attention. The smile disappeared. "We have to get out of here. This way," Matt shouted on a cough over the roar of the fire. He crawled for the door with Lara right behind him. He fought the urge to look back and make sure she was there. They had been in countless fires together. Despite everything, he knew she would be there.

The stairs burned, a wall of flames leaping toward them.

They didn't have a choice. He held out a hand. She nodded and grabbed his hand. They ran for the stairs and jumped.

Lara sat on the curb with a blanket around her shoulders. Shudders still ran through her even though it was a warm summer night. She held the oxygen mask to her face and breathed deeply.

It had been close.

Too close. Matt had risked his life to save hers. He was sitting a couple of feet away on the back end of the ambulance. He hadn't been severely injured, but he had multiple second-degree burns and cuts and bruises on his hands where he fought to free her from the closet. They would both be monitored for smoke inhalation damage.

Across the parking lot, Cruse Conyers packed a hand-cuffed Owen Burke into the back of an SBPD cruiser. He'd been caught with the duffel of money as he was leaving the building. His loyal sidekick, the chemistry whiz kid Baxter, had already agreed to roll over on him in return for protection inside prison.

B shift paramedic True Paulson lifted Lara's hand to check the pulse oximeter reading. "Hey, O_2 is 94 and your heart rate's hovering around 90. I'd say you're doing better."

She rolled her eyes up at him and pulled the mask away from her face. "I want a Diet Coke."

He grinned, dual dimples creasing his cheeks. "I want a chocolate lava cake. You can't always get what you want. Oh, wait, isn't that a song?"

True walked back to the bus, humming the tune. Firefighters were so obnoxious. She adored them, each and every one.

Matt pushed away from the medics at the ambulance. "I'm fine, guys, really."

He stomped the three feet over to her and sat down on the curb beside her. True's partner followed with the oxygen and hooked it over Matt's mouth and nose.

"Persistent, isn't he?" Matt said through the mask. His face was sooty and cut and he had a burn on his cheek from falling debris, but he looked so beautiful to her.

She shivered again.

"Cold?" He pulled the blanket up from behind her and anchored it around her shoulders.

"Not really." She held the blanket closed with her finger and shuddered again. Her eyes found his. "Thank you for coming for me."

"Are you kidding me? If I lost you, I'd have to train another partner and do you know how long—" He let the words trail off. "I can't do this, Lara. I can't pretend that things are the same. I love you and if anything had happened to you, it would've killed me."

Her throat, already cloggy from the soot, began to ache, unshed tears locked up inside.

He pulled on the edge of the blanket to turn her toward him. "Did you mean what you said?"

She took a deep breath. It was now or never. It was standing at the top of that staircase and knowing if you didn't jump you were going to die. If she didn't take the risk, their story ended here. And she wasn't about to let that happen.

She pushed her mask up to her forehead. "People say a lot of things in the heat of the moment."

Matt didn't say anything, but his dark eyes seared into hers. She leaned forward and pushed his mask up to the top of his head.

Her blanket dropped off her shoulders, but she didn't reach for it. Instead she reached for his, grabbing each side of it with her fists and pulling him forward so that he was inches away from her face. "I meant *every* word. I love you, Matt Clark. Now, will you please go out on a date with me?"

He didn't move, but a suspicious moisture formed in his eyes. And since she was holding on to him anyway, she pulled him the rest of the way in, pressing her lips to his. He dropped his blanket and wrapped his arms around her.

A wolf whistle sounded from the direction of the ambulance. Matt broke the kiss, laughing.

Then he slid his hands into her hair and pulled her close again. The flashing red lights of the ambulance and the police cars, the bustle of the fire and crime scene disappeared when she looked into his eyes. "You name the time and the day. I promise, it's a date."

EPILOGUE

The boat dropped them off at the end of the pier on the small Gulf-front island. During the day, the island beach was crowded with tourists, but normally, the park closed at sundown. The sea-soft breeze lifted Lara's hair, the waves softly shushing as they rolled in to the shore.

As the boat pulled away, Lara turned to Matt. "How did you arrange this?"

"I have my resources." A mysterious smile tipped the corner of his mouth. He reached under a bench and pulled out a picnic basket.

"Dinner at Les Trois Frères, now this? You're definitely spoiling me." She'd felt very, very cherished as Matt had opened doors for her and pulled out the chair at dinner, even standing up for her when she'd gone to the powder room.

While she'd taken care of a lot of people

in her life, she'd never felt like she could let go of the choke hold that she had on her life. But with Matt, she could. Somehow she knew steady, *steadfast* Matt could be trusted.

It was like being in a room full of smoke, lungs burning, vision fading, and suddenly— *finally*—being able to take a breath of pure, clean air.

He was a gift. One she'd almost missed because of her fear.

Matt cracked open the picnic basket and pulled out a thermos of coffee and an insulated bag. "Diet Coke for the lady?"

"You thought of everything. Maybe in a few minutes?"

"Let's go for a walk." They stepped into the silky-soft sand. Gleaming white in the moonlight, it stretched for what seemed like miles.

Matt slid his hand around hers, linking their fingers. "I've decided to stay with the fire department."

"What?" Lara put a hand on his chest, stopping him midstep. Little white sand crabs skittered in front of them, dodging the surf as its fingers reached long. "Why? You've worked so hard."

He smiled, and in the moonlight, there was

a sparkle in his eye. "I realized it wasn't really my dream to be in law enforcement. I thought it would make my dad happy. And then there's the fact that the chief of the fire department wouldn't let me go. Apparently, he has plans for me."

Lara laughed. "Wow. This has been a big week for you."

She had no idea.

Matt stopped walking and just looked over the water. It was a gorgeous night. Outside the lights of the town, the stars seemed to try to outshine each other in the sky, a glittering array of diamonds. He couldn't help but feel the night was somehow magical, somehow perfect.

He'd waited so long for this night to happen and now that it had, it was even better than his imagination.

"Matt, look." Her voice held a note of awe. As he looked where she pointed, he saw it. The ocean water shimmered with light, every soft crest, every easy breaker. "Phosphorescence. I knew it happened, but I've never seen it."

Her eyes shone as she looked into his. "I've never had a night like this."

He pulled her close, fitting her just there under his chin. "I love you."

"I love you, too." She buried her face in his chest, glossy blond hair sliding down to cover her cheek. "I still can't believe I'm saying it."

Matt reached in his pocket and pulled out an even bigger glimmer than the ocean. At the first glimpse, she gasped and backed away, her hands flying up to cover her mouth.

He went in heart-first, the only way he knew how. "Lara, I know we haven't been dating or anything, but you've seen me at my best and my worst. We've gone through really tough times together and some good times, too. I can't think of anything in my life that wouldn't be better with you by my side." He held the ring out to her. "I'd be honored if you would be my wife."

"*Oh*. Oh, Matt. Are you sure?"

"Are you kidding me? I'm standing here with a ring in my hand and my heart in my throat about to die, thinking you're about to turn me down." His hand shook as he held the ring.

She held out her left hand, a beautiful smile on her face as she nodded her yes. "Spend the rest of your life with me, Matt Clark. *I dare you*."

* * * * *

Love the men and women of
EMERALD COAST 911?
Look for CSI Maria Fuentes's story,
"Christmas Target,"
in the Christmas collection
HOLIDAY HAVOC
in November 2010,
only from Love Inspired Suspense.

Dear Reader,

Matt and Lara's story in *Flashpoint* was inspired by a single conversation they had in another book. From their body language, another character could tell he had feelings for her and she wanted to protect herself. But why? How do friends fall in love, especially when one of them is dead set against it?

Then I met Lara's mom and sister and I knew that it wasn't who Lara was—it wasn't even who they were—that kept Lara from a relationship with Matt. It was who she *believed* she was. And sometimes that's even harder to overcome. She had to learn to listen to God's voice rather than her own, to accept God's grace as a free gift—and Matt's grace as a friend—before she could accept his love.

Fighting fires was no problem. Stepping out to trust another person with her heart? Big-time scary. Good thing God is a big-time God!

Thanks for picking up *Flashpoint*. Please look for CSI Maria Fuentes's story, "Christmas Target," coming in November! For more information on upcoming books, please visit www.stephanienewtonbooks.com or e-mail me at newtonwriter@gmail.com. I'd love to hear from you!

All the best,

Stephanie Newton

QUESTIONS FOR DISCUSSION

1. Lara doesn't want anyone to know about her family. Why?

2. Is it rational for Lara not to want people to know her secrets? Why or why not?

3. Has anyone ever reacted badly when he or she found out the "real truth" about you? How did it make you feel?

4. Matt is becoming an arson investigator because he thinks it will make his dad proud. Is this a good decision?

5. Although Matt has some issues with approval, he has an amazingly strong faith. Where did Matt learn his faith?

6. Why is Lara so stunned when Matt reaches out to Emmy?

7. What does Matt tell Emmy that is so shocking to Lara?

8. What does Lara learn about Matt's family

that makes it easier for her to understand him (and easier to forgive her own family)?

9. How does Lara's relationship with her mom really begin to heal with a birthday party for a little boy?

10. Why was it so special to Lara that Matt treated her like "one of the guys"?

11. What does Lara mean when she says, "It was easier to take the dare than to tell the truth"?

12. When Lara dresses like her sister, she sees all the things in herself that she's been trying to hide from Matt. How is that any different than feeling like you don't belong somewhere or feeling insecure about something in your past or in your life? Is it?

LARGER-PRINT BOOKS!

**GET 2 FREE
LARGER-PRINT NOVELS
PLUS 2 FREE
MYSTERY GIFTS**

Love Inspired.
SUSPENSE
RIVETING INSPIRATIONAL ROMANCE

Larger-print novels are now available...